SECRETS OF A PASTOR'S WIFE 2

BILLIE MIFF

URBAN AESOP PRESENTS

Email: Urbanaesop@gmail.com

Facebook: Free Said Salaam or Black Ink Publications

Cover design: Adriane Hall

CHAPTER ONE

Carl

"Put your hands where I can see them! On the dashboard! Put them on the dashboard!"

The patrol officer's voice boomed through the crisp night air. I couldn't believe I had been so careless, speeding through that intersection. I admit, my mind had been swirling with thoughts about the shocking occurrence at church this morning. The embarrassment I experienced in front of the whole congregation was not only humiliating, but irreversible.

My son—well, this man who claims to be my son—stood squarely in front of me, looked me in the eyes, and called me *Dad*. Astonished by his boldness, I found it hard to recover. My message spattered a bit, which made everyone take notice. I believe this was his intention, to make a scene so that he could have the stage. I wasn't going to allow him the control he desired, so I politely asked him to take a seat and we could discuss whatever he wished after the service.

We talked in private, with him telling me his whole story, from start to the point where he stepped into my church. I quickly reminded him of the responsibility bestowed upon me, after which he quickly reminded me of an obligation to the truth. His mission was to be the deliverer of the truth. We both had a purpose; I just didn't understand his, and he didn't understand mine.

One thing was evident: we did share the same blood, his features proved that. Hearing his story made me remember his mother and those sordid memories that came with her. I did recall our relationship; it was brief and we did have sex. I just didn't know she was pregnant. Our breakup fell on bad terms, putting agreeable distance between us. She never tried to contact me to tell me she was carrying my child. Our lives moved forward in different directions, and I never looked back.

When he revealed that she passed away, it did hurt a little. Any time you connect with someone and they leave this earth, it will have some sort of effect on you. I had no idea she left behind a son. Surely, the impact it had on him was tremendous; so much that he spiraled into a lift of drug addiction. Overcoming those odds made him stronger, making him the man he was today.

For me, it was like I failed with his mother and, ultimately, with him. Now, I had an even bigger challenge:

trying to explain all of this to Sandra. It took years for her to understand my reason for adopting Chloe without consulting with her. We both agreed to wanting another child; the opportunity presented itself, so I took advantage of it. I thought she'd be ecstatic about the addition of another little girl, especially with the relationship she had with Reecie.

In all honesty, I realized that a natural connection between mother and daughter would be hard to compete with. From birth, I felt Sandra's love dissipate, slowly being rechanneled to Sharice. Meanwhile, I was left with a void I tried desperately to replace. With Chloe, I figured I'd be solving two issues at once. The way I saw it now was not at all what I figured. Sometimes, your plans and God's didn't always match up.

I should've told Sandra long ago that there was a chance I could have a child out there, but then again, how was I to know? The circumstances were cloudy, times were different, and things were moving fast. This may not be the night to put this out there to her or anyone else. I was considered a public figure; not to mention, my aspirations to become a Bishop one day. Having a dysfunctional family was not a good look.

Getting a speeding ticket was definitely not in the plans either, so maybe he would show some compassion if I tried to reason with him. Looking through the rearview mirror, I could see him gather his hat and step out of his squad car aggressively, blue lights flashing furiously. In the light of everything that has been going on recently with police officers, my antenna was up, watching his movements carefully.

The moment he stepped out, I noticed he was Caucasian. Race mattered; believe me, I was sure he had profiled me as well. As he barked his orders, I remained calm.

"My hands are on the dash, Sir," I tried to give him reassurance.

"Shut up! Did I ask you to talk?" With one hand on his holster, he unlatched his weapon as he came closer to my door. My window was already down, so he could see what he needed to see. I wanted him to know that I wasn't a threat in any way.

"I need to see your license and registration. With your right hand, slowly retrieve those items. If you make any false or sudden movements, I will be forced to shoot you."

"I'm a pastor of a church, officer," I decided to mention, reaching for my wallet from the console.

"So. And is there a logical reason for you to speed through that light back there? Are you in a hurry to meet Jesus? Because driving recklessly puts your life and others in danger." I handed him the items without a response. He looked at me, then at the articles in his hand. "Please step out of the car, Mr. Andrews."

"May I ask why, Sir?"

"Because I said so! Any other questions?"

"Are you wearing a body cam?" Didn't quite know where that came from, but it was worth asking.

"What! Get out of the goddamn car before I get mad! Do I have a body cam," he mumbled under his breath. He pulled his weapon out as I exited the car, hands raised.

"Put your hands on the trunk while I go run your information. Don't move," he shouted, as if I was a boy who warranted such correction. I was still dressed in my suit, tie loosened a bit, but dressed conservatively, no doubt. Definitely not a threat in my eyes; however, it was his perception that mattered at the moment.

All I could think about was the recent events involving black males and routine traffic stops gone completely wrong. His tone reflected someone who was mad for no reason; the result could be him taking action based on emotion. In his position, that was never good; the outcome never favored the civilian. Every life mattered; tonight, my black life mattered most.

It seemed like an eternity for him to go through what was usually a formality; nowadays, running a license plate and ID took a mere stroke of a keypad. The anxiety came by having my back turned to his car, lights flashing behind me. The unknown was what opened the door to fear. His car door swung open, which ignited an uneasiness in my stomach. It was just my luck that there was no traffic going or coming that could witness an injustice if it were to take place. The silence was broken with the stern walk of his approach.

"Turn and face me, Mr. Andrews." I did as I was told, looking the man of the law in the eye. A haunting quiet filled the air.

"Is everything alright. Officer?" As the question escaped my lips, I saw his eyes change from confident to submissive. His posture transformed from strong and authoritative to frail and vulnerable in an instant. In a twist of fate, he collapsed to the ground, gasping for air.

I was no medical expert; however, I did know when someone was suffering. Looking at his name tag, I got his name so I could address him properly.

"Officer Glascow!" I called out to him, receiving no verbal response. His eyes told another story. He peered up at me, pleading for help. I leaned down to listen to his breathing; it was labored. I wondered if he was asthmatic, the way he was wheezing.

"I...I need—," he could barely utter a word. Doing what came natural, I helped him. Like so many in my congregation, I helped him. Like the sick I went to visit in the hospitals, I helped. I prayed and did my best to help him by grabbing the radio attached to his shoulder and called in.

"Officer down! Officer down! Need assistance!" the radio squawked its response. A few moments later, an officer's reply came over the radio, asking for Officer Glascow's location and condition. I told him we were somewhere in Montgomery County, but was too panicked to give an exact direction to where we could be found.

Luckily, we lived in a technological age. He told me to call his cell and GPS would track our location.

While we waited, I propped him up in order for him to have a better breathing angle. He was apparently weak, and his eyes fought to keep open. I couldn't tell what was troubling him; I felt helpless. Prayer seemed like the only recourse at this point, so I knelt down next to him on the pavement. I closed my eyes and spoke audibly to my God to please step in and give me strength I knew I didn't have. I needed Him to display a healing power beyond measure.

The thought of this routine traffic stop ending tragically did cross my mind, just not in this way.

"Don't try to talk, be still, help is on the way," I said, comforting him when he began moving his mouth to speak. In the distance, I could hear the sirens coming from the ambulance or patrol cars; whichever arrived first, I would be relieved. Looking for a blessing of my own, I became a welcome blessing to Officer Glascow.

Just as the paramedics pulled up, Officer Glascow lost consciousness. He was loaded onto a stretcher and moved to the back of the ambulance, where he was hooked up to a series of tubes. Something inside told me to stay until the scene settled down. As I stood watching the commotion around his car and all the medical staff scurrying to get him secured, I noticed something near my left rear wheel.

On the ground was a piece of paper with some official writing on it. At the bottom was Officer Glascow's signature and badge information. I looked up just as they were closing the ambulance doors. I caught a glimpse of the offi-cer's eyes looking back at me. He wrote me a ticket for speeding, something he thought was going to damage my character as a Pastor. Little did he know, what ended up happening gave way to show my true character as a Pastor beyond all obstacles. I was still in a position to do God's work in the midst of troubled circumstances. I was chal-lenged and rose to the test. I loved watching God work.

CHAPTER TWO

COOKIE

His hands on my body were as soothing as massage therapy. Every inch of me tingled with the touch of his fingers on my skin. I closed my eyes and imagined all the things I wanted to do to him. He took his time with me, like I was in need of intensive care and he knew all the right places that would get a reaction.

I was in desperate need of attention; my body craved it like air to breathe. Maybe I'd been suffering from deprivation because even his body heat did something to me. I couldn't help but to hold on to his shoulders when he got near a spot that made me shudder. It had been so long since I'd been caressed like this, I was almost frightened by how good it felt.

Being nude in front of him didn't embarrass me at all. I was more in awe of his physique and how his hard-toned frame contrasted my softness. It felt like a natural mesh; my flesh mixing with his made it a perfect combination. Our heat together was combustible. There was no need to extinguish it; the desire was to keep it burning.

He tasted me, sampling portions of my skin. I thought he may have lost himself at the buffet the way he traveled from delicacies to desserts without coming up for air. When his breath neared my treasure, I became flooded with emotion and then poured out my appreciation in a tidal wave, overflowing the dam that had been holding it back. My moans couldn't be contained any longer; the ecstasy was revealed in my facial expressions.

Then he entered my after much anticipation. As if the foreplay wasn't enough, he took me to a new level of passion that I could never have reached if it hadn't been for his thorough exploration. I welcomed him willingly, submitting to whatever he desired to do with me. He granted my wishes for more, going farther as if reading my thoughts. The echoes bouncing off the walls haunted me, and then I realized that they were the sounds of my own voice morphed by pleasure. Transformed by his nature, I didn't recognize myself or my actions. The things I did, I hadn't done in a long time. The mood made the experience memorable.

Climaxes came and went, then came again, bringing me to the point of exhaustion. After what seemed like hours, the two of us collapsed in a pool of our own perspiration. Our pores were open, taking in the cool air which we desperately needed to lower our temperatures. There was a slight chance that a fire could be quickly ignited with just one touch in the right place. I moved a safe distance away from him in fear of that reality. When chemistry was strong like ours, it could be hard to resist temptation.

Looking deeply into his brown eyes, I saw things he had been hiding. Without a spoken word, the communication between us was loud and clear. Through body language, I understood the emptiness he had felt; time away left him lonely, a man who was in need of completeness. I felt a sense of sorrow for him. Trying to imagine his struggles was nearly impossible, yet I did my best to empathize. I hoped my presence alone would help the healing process. In the meantime, I offered my touch, my affection, myself as a vessel for him to channel his energy. I retracted to his comforting arms, allowing his warmth to shield me from my cold world. With him, it seemed easier to deal with my problems. With him, I felt free.

"Cookie! Cookie!" The pierce of Maxine's voice broke me out of that special place in my mind I had withdrawn to. I had gotten pretty good lately at finding an escape by going to these imaginary retreats. I just didn't realize I was so far gone. Max had excused herself to take an important phone call, which created space for my mind to roam.

"I'm sorry, Max."

"Wow! Girl, wherever you just were, please take me

with you next time." Now embarrassment filled my expression.

"I'm good."

"Oh, I can see that. If looks could tell a story, you just showed me a bestseller. Where was your mind at?"

"In a faraway place. Somewhere I needed to be at the moment."

"Nothing wrong with a fantasy every now and then. Nice for a man to be able to take you there." My distant look caused her to inquire.

"Please tell me it was your husband that was in your fantasy?" Silence was the only answer I could come up with. "Cookie?"

"What can I say? I mean, I wish we were in that kind of space, just not so."

"If not Carl, then who?" Again, I wasn't able to utter a word, which was enough of an answer for her to deduce what was going on. "Really, Cookie? Adrian?" My uncomfortable blushing confirmed what she thought.

"Can we change the subject? So, what was so important on the phone that you had to interrupt our very important time together?"

"I'll let you off the hook this time. I know our time is valuable, but that call was a pressing issue. My lawyer wanted to discuss my options in my case."

"I almost forgot that you still had to go to court on that charge."

"Cookie, all you did was bond me out, that didn't make everything go away."

"I know."

"Besides, I still have to repay you the $25,000 you put up. That kind of money doesn't grow on trees."

"Hell, what kind of money does? Anyway, you just work with your lawyer and fight. Let me worry about the money." Truth be told, I didn't have a clue on how I was going to get the money back to the church. I was trusting Sister Allen's ability to keep the funds hidden long enough for me to come up with a solution. She told me about her meeting with Carl and him questioning her about some issues he had discovered. She said at first, she was scared he noticed what she had done, but it appeared she was in the clear. He just wanted her to be prepared in the event of an audit. That just told me to tighten up and get the money back as fast as possible; I had to get her out of hot water.

"I feel like the walls are closing in on me," she said, letting out a sigh. "The court case doesn't concern me as much as having to deal with those thugs who gave me that hush money. I'm sure they're not happy with their key witness perjuring herself, damaging their hopes of getting their man off. Personally, I wish I had never seen anything."

"But you did, Max. You can't dwell on that. Just focus on one thing at a time, trust in God for everything else."

"Thank you, Cookie. You're a good woman and a great friend."

"I'm glad someone sees that."

My sessions with Maxine always brought me a sense of peace. It was a shame I had to go outside my home to find solace; it should be the exact opposite. This world, however, was not all cookie-cutter perfect; sometimes, what you think is a model for peace was really a haven for turmoil. That was the reality I lived in daily.

I think I need a vacation. If there was a way I could escape for just a brief moment, maybe a week or two, that would do wonders for my psyche. However, at this particular time in my life, with the whirlwind of events going on, getting away just wouldn't be possible. My only release was through my ministry. Empowering women, young and old, was exhilarating and gave me fulfillment.

This foray at the prison was something new, but equally as rewarding to the spirit. Watching the brothers inside express their love for the word had been refreshing. I could tell the rest of our church family that traveled to Lofton was as surprised as I was at the turnout, and the reception we received on each of our two trips there. For that two-hour period, those guys in there were no different than us out here. It put us in the same place spiritually.

Getting my spiritual balance back has been imperative to me lately. I realized after being in the trunk of that car, things in life could go left at a moment's notice. I meant no harm to him and was just doing what I had to do to protect

Chloe. However, going into his territory could've been perceived as a threat, and although I felt like being kidnapped was a bit extreme, I couldn't say that I blamed him. I was just grateful for my life being spared.

Chloe was growing into her own woman. With only one more year of high school left, she was going to have to make sound decisions and deal with the consequences. That particularly went for her choices in men. She definitely didn't want to start her journey into adulthood by entering into bad relationships. Patterns began like that and were hard to break. Trust me, I was only teaching her out of experience.

She was just so rebellious and combative when it came to me. It was almost as though the way I was parenting was offensive in her eyes, yet Carl would get father of the year if it were up to her. Such a contrast, considering we tried to approach her initially with a united front. It became divided when Carl decided to undermine me and cater to her every wish. To me, that sort of spoiling only presented problems in the future.

Fast forward to the present. Now, because of our division, we were having a tough time reeling her in. Her focus seemed to be primarily on Gabriel and how she was going to spend her life after she left our house. I wondered if she even knew the side of Gabriel that I saw. He seemed like the kind of man who thrived on power and control, and the fact that she is a grade younger than him put her in a vulnerable position. Once she relinquished control to him, it would be nearly impossible to get her back.

I was worried about Reecie. My hopes were that she didn't view Chloe's behavior as something to mimic. She was very impressionable and it was only natural for younger sisters to emulate their older siblings. I tried hard to protect my baby from the world, but the influence was all around her. It was inevitable that nature took its course. I was just glad that, in Reecie's eyes, I was still Mother Nature.

CHAPTER THREE

Adrian

I couldn't believe it when I heard the news. At first, I figured it was just a rumor, and then Pam confirmed it to be true. After all, she should know; when it comes to staff, their version was usually most accurate. We had gotten so close that she took any opportunity to pull me aside to hit me with the latest gossip from one of their meetings. I was in a privileged position to get information that no one else could. The main thing I had to keep in mind was not to run back to the dorm spilling the beans that would violate her trust in me, which was rule number one when dealing with staff members: always secure the trust.

"It's true, he is gay," Pam said to me in the confidence of her office. We kind of suspected Officer Turner of having homosexual tendencies due to the way he would throw mini tantrums around his co-workers when things weren't going his way. But he had a lot of people fooled because he was always seen talking and flirting with the women around the compound. It went both ways; the women found him attractive and went out of their way to show him attention.

Being gay and working at a male correctional facility was like putting a fox in a chicken coop and telling him not to touch. Eventually, something inside was going to be triggered and the urges would be explored. In Officer Turner's case, and fortunately for him, he got exposed off duty. The flip side to him being off the prison grounds was that a secret life could be hidden. Thomas Turner was living wild and carefree, not thinking that someone would be watching. In today's society, everyone was watching and phones were always on, waiting on the chance to catch someone in the wrong.

It just so happened, he was in the wrong place at the wrong time. Thomas Turner, or Tina as he was referred to that night when he was in drag, was lost in his own underworld. Standing outside of a LGBT club, he got picked up for solicitation when a lurking police officer witnessed the interaction between Tina and an unknown man in a sports car. Money was exchanged and that's what caused the officer to take action. To add insult to injury, the incident was caught on camera and posted on social media, labeled as *Good Night Turned Bad*. With all the attention drawn to the viral posting, it was later discovered that the female in question was actually a man, one Thomas Turner, Officer Thomas Turner of Lofton State Prison.

As an officer here at the prison, Turner was well liked by inmates. Most knew how he was, yet still treated him as if all was normal. There was one inmate who made a connection and worked it to his benefit. He was worried about what the public thought; his motive was to win, regardless of the consequences.

Stanley Hardwick, or Hardy as we called him, was what we called a finesser, one who knew how to play a position to get what he wanted. He could finesse anyone out of anything if given a chance. One time, he got $1000.00 from a guy by working his game. This young, white inmate was in the market to buy a phone. Well Hardy, playing the role of the good guy, decided to be the mediator and help the young kid out. He gained his trust by making him comfortable with the deal and the players involved. For a white guy in the system where they were considered a minority, it was extremely hard for him to own anything of value, so finding allies was a must.

When it came time for the transaction to take place, Hardy took control of the deal with the kid's consent. $500.00 was the price initially quoted for the smartphone, which he made seem like a steal. In his haste, the money was sent to a card that was designated by Hardy. The swindle went into play when he mentioned a complication with the transfer. Hardy convinced the kid that there must've been an error in the way it was sent, and that he should try it again. Without a second thought, the kid got on the phone and had his family produce another $500.00 after fully explaining what Hardy had told him. When it was confirmed that the money had arrived, Hardy gave the kid a phone; one problem, the phone was a dud.

Hardy got away with $1000.00, and the young kid got stuck with a phone he could never use. There was no way for him to correct the situation. That would've required him to either confront Hardy or the man selling the merchandise. He didn't want either option. Being a Caucasian in the system meant that sometimes, you were put in no-win situations.

That was a position Hardy had Officer Turner in. When they encountered each other, Officer Turner was working his dorm. Everyone was giving Turner the business when they found out he had homosexual tendencies, but not Hardy; he used that to his advantage. While the others created an enemy with Turner, Hardy chose to befriend him.

They got close and Turner started taking a liking to him. Once Hardy recognized the attraction, he sprang into the driver's seat. Now Hardy wasn't gay, or at least had never been rumored to be gay. He hadn't even been grouped up in that classification like most guys that had done a lot of time and messed around. No, Hardy was being strategic in his approach. He figured if he did the opposite of what everyone else was doing, then he would be accepted; it worked.

Acting was the hardest part of Hardy's plan. He had to pretend to be interested in Turner, which was some work, but worth doing. Most wouldn't even think of going there, afraid of what people would think. Hardy, however, was focused on one thing: getting to the money. When Turner mentioned, in one of their private conversations, that he was having some issues with paying a couple of his bills, Hardy pounced on the opportunity to offer help.

"Look Turner, I don't mean to shed light on your unfortunate situation, but it had me thinking and I may have a temporary solution for you."

"I'm listening."

This was where things got tricky. No matter how close he thought they were, Hardy was about to cross the line and had to be careful. Gaining Turner's trust was key, but he was risking him flipping the script and citing him for an offense. Hardy remained confident in his plan.

"There's a way you can make some extra cash, but it's gonna require you to trust me. I got you, though." There was an uncomfortable silence before Turner responded.

"I already know how y'all move in here, believe me, I've had officers to get money."

"And?'

"Just wasn't the right situation, wasn't feeling the guy

at the time. He seemed kinda shifty. Plus his movements were shaky, hanging with a bunch of dudes all the time. I felt like at any moment, he would run his mouth, so I pulled back." To Hardy, that sounded like rejection; a gleam of hope appeared in Turner's eye. A change of heart came next. "But I'm willing to hear what you got, what you talking about?" It almost shocked Hardy to hear Turner's openness.

"Well, I got a man out there on the street that is willing to get on the road and meet you."

"So you already had me as your target, damn Hardwick."

"Hold up, before you jump to conclusions. My man asked me if I had someone in here that could pick up some work he has. He said he'd pay them $1500.00 to meet him and bring it in to me." Turner heard the dollar amount and initially became interested, forgetting all about his irritation.

"What exactly would I be bringing, and when is all of this supposed to go down?"

"Here's his number; he'll discuss the details when you call. You decide when is the best time to come in with it and get it to me. There's no pressure from my end."

Officer Turner took a day or so to think about the proposition before he made the call. There were actually a couple of events that led to him making the decision. The first thing happened when he came to work the next morning and the supervisors on his shift were giving him a hard time about some paperwork, then began harassing him about his court procedure. It had him so frustrated that all he could think about was getting home after his shift, relaxing, and getting a drink. When he got home, he was faced with darkness; his lights had been cut off.

Before his phone was cut off next, he made the call to make arrangements with Hardy's guy on the street. They met and, just as it was offered, $750.00 cash was handed to Turner along with a package containing cigarettes, marijuana, and pills. The other half of the money would be paid once the delivery was successfully made to Hardy. As long as business was handled properly on both ends, a good deal of money could be made.

Turner saw this as a way to solve all his problems; it also made coming to work a whole lot more bearable. He intended to honor his word to Hardy and continue in their partnership. Because Hardy was a veteran and moved with the skill of an undercover agent, no one suspected a thing. All financial transactions were exchanged on the outside, and Hardy constructed a team that kept him out of the spotlight.

The commissary money that was made on the inside was used to get his soldiers to move product from point A to point B. Any overflow was funneled into dorms that did a lot of gambling and used as banks to fund their habits. Hardy was always thinking, covering for every contingency. However, he didn't account for the snitches; one in particular. Big B was notorious for seeing too much, hearing too much, and knowing too much. From prison to prison, he always found his way in the mix of things. There was suspicion that the administration had him in place to get intel. With his resume of informing, it was a wonder he hadn't been seriously hurt or even worse, killed.

Without repercussion, Big B had the liberty to do and say what he pleased. This had caused many an empire to go down big. Hardy called himself being extra careful; however, it was Turner who slipped and let his movements get noticed. Once again, Big B was in the right place at the right time. Officer Turner had a system with men in place to deliver the product to Hardy. It would travel from one area to the next undetected, where it was then picked up by a designated person at a specific checkpoint and supervised by someone he trusted.

Everything moved like clockwork, all except one minor detail: a bystander who just happened to be near the checkpoint. Big B was coming out of the inmate barbershop, heading toward the gate that led to his building. What looked normal to most people appeared out of place to Big B. His antennas were up, paying more attention to his surroundings. What he witnessed was the transport of a laundry cart to Hardy's building as he left from the gate. The cart being out at that time of the day was what alerted Big B. So before he entered his dormitory, he kept his eye on the cart's destination and then put two and two together from there.

All of this transpired after three months of doing

business. Officer Turner and Hardy had a decent run of it before it all came to an end. Big B couldn't stand for something to be going on without him knowing about it. It wasn't even a matter of him wanting in; he was just the kind of guy who didn't want to see anyone else win. Hardy was picked up and put in lockdown, pending an investigation. They didn't catch him with anything, but the suspicion alone made them come and detain him. Big B's reputation spoke volumes and was enough to do the damage. Turner was never named as a suspect. Hardy remained solid and kept his mouth closed the whole fifty-four days he spent in the hole. The administration got tired of him being silent and finally let him out. By that time, Big B was gone, transferred to another facility. He, most likely, was waiting for his next big score.

"When are you coming down here again?" I asked Cookie, because I was starting to miss her.

"Our group was due in there this weekend coming up."

"Good."

"You say that like you miss me or something."

"I kinda miss that face and the smile. Oh, and—"

"Okay, you can stop right there. Remember, I am a lady of the church," she said jokingly.

"I know that you haven't always been a lady of the church."

"And how do you know that?"

"Because everyone transforms from something. You were a caterpillar before you became a butterfly."

"So, I'm a butterfly to you?"

"Well, put it this way: when I see you, I see your colors glowing brightly, wings spread ready to fly."

"You don't know just how right you are."

CHAPTER FOUR

Carl

I was tired of going through the same cycle with these women in this household. My wife was distant and seemed to be focused on other things instead of trying to fix us. We barely spoke; in fact, I found myself texting her phone more if she was in another part of the house,—that's how we communicated. I didn't know where we went wrong. Was it me or her? Who was the cause of our problems? Whoever was to blame, we needed to find a solution.

What I did know was I made the money and provided for the roof over our heads. At some point, they needed to appreciate what was going on around here. My church family was much more considerate of my efforts. When I was there, everything seemed to fall in place. I didn't encounter friction or the frigidness that was present in my home. To me, there was something unnatural about it. Most marriages had genuine warmth that surrounded them; ours, however, had the cold feeling of a meat locker.

I was determined to get my family back on track. I didn't know what it was going to take, but I was willing to figure it out. The question was, whether Sandra was onboard or not. At times, she seemed genuinely interested in family matters, especially when it came to our daughters. As far as I was concerned, that relationship was important. I just wished our relationship was as equally important to her. She must realize that I loved her, even if it didn't feel like it.

I have my way of showing love; it may not be traditional, but it works for me. Ask my congregation; I give and receive love on a daily basis. They give me everything I miss at home.

At the church, I feel like I have purpose. People rely on me, and I try to give them the best of me whenever possible. Like last week, when Sister Price came to me seeking advice about her marriage. She suspected her husband of cheating on her. Sister Lola Price is one of our faithful members; she is also one of the younger sisters in Christ. In her mid '30s, she decided to rededicate her life and chose our church family as her place of fellowship.

Her husband, Ashton, is the antithesis of Lola and rarely comes to service. When he does attend, it's at Lola's request and his boredom is evident. After his inability to stay awake in the services he did attend, she regretted asking him to be a part of something she enjoyed so much. Ashton began to find other interests to fill his time while Lola attended Bible study on Wednesday and Friday evening worship and praise night.

He started to frequent strip clubs in downtown D.C. The more time Lola spent in church, the more Ashton felt obligated to play the streets. He saw it as a cure for his loneliness. Distance crept into their marriage and caused a divide. It wasn't long before Ashton's late nights began to irritate Lola to the point where she felt she had to confront her husband. She feared this approach, thinking it would push him further away. She was right; Ashton went from coming in late to not coming home at all.

As a wife, Lola was not only concerned and disappointed, she was also embarrassed to think if any of this got out to the congregation, she would be the laughing stock. Her suspicion led her to follow Ashton one night after he failed to come home at a decent hour. To be a young couple experiencing these issues had her worried about the future of their marriage. This is what fueled her drive to find out what exactly was going on with Ashton.

She watched and waited as his truck sat in the parking lot of his favorite strip club, *Fun Bunz*. Time didn't matter to her. An hour and a half passed before Ashton and a group of guys exited the establishment. In the midst of the crowd was a scantily-dressed woman walking beside Ashton. When the group separated, Ashton and the woman strolled toward his truck giggling.

They pulled off in a hurry, catching the first highway out of the city. It nearly took top speed to keep up with them before they exited into Silver Spring, finally stopping at a Holiday Inn. Lola stood nearby unnoticed as Ashton and his new friend checked in. When they entered the elevator and she was assured that they were gone, she sauntered out toward the revolving doors leading to the parking lot. Her body language spoke a thousand words; emotions poured out through tears and angry words she swore to give up in her newfound righteousness.

What she was experiencing was deep hurt. Watching the love of her life walk beside another woman in a hotel was about as low as it got. She wondered where their marriage had gone wrong. Her connection with her husband was weakening as they grew apart, like the east is to the west, and she worried about their future.

I had a soft spot for our younger members, feeling as though they needed a little extra guidance. So I tended to assign selected Deacons or other officials to mentor them toward a stronger walk. My prayers were that they considered counseling together, as a couple, or at least individually. My heart went out to Sister Price; she deserved the fullness of life.

"Pastor Andrews, your 5:30 appointment is here, where are you?"

Mrs. Chandler, my secretary, is always on me about being late. I applauded her attention to punctuality; she did her best to keep me on point. However, this rare occasion of tardiness was due to the unexpected news that just had to be tended to.

I got a call about my daughter, Chloe, from her school's guidance department. Evidently, she had been skipping classes, leaving her status for graduation in jeopardy. After hearing her counselor recount the number of times she missed class, I decided that Ms. Chloe and I had to have a father-daughter talk. My mind couldn't process the thought of where she could actually be going when she was supposed to be in school. There were so many dangers out there, something tragic could happen and we wouldn't even know about it.

"Mrs. Chandler, I'm on my way. I had a pressing call I had to take." I'd deal with Chloe later. As long as she was upstairs, she was unaware of the utter rage I had within. I'd leave her there while I was gone; that way, I could get my thoughts together.

When I arrived at the church, I noticed something different about my parking spot. The sign that notified the public that the spot was reserved for the Pastor was covered with a black bag. I thought it was weird, but waited until I went inside before I questioned anyone. What I did wonder was why my sign had been singled out and all of the others were left undisturbed.

My office was organized to perfection, one of the many qualities I admired about Mrs. Chandler. I didn't know if it was a case of OCD or administrative assistant experience from previous employers that had her skills in cleaning up to par. Whatever the reason, I was glad to have her. She'd been a godsend.

The minutes from yesterday's meeting were in the outbox, waiting to be filed. Also, there was the expense report for the trips to Lofton Prison. One of Sandra's responsibilities was to write a thorough report and to submit an expense breakdown. That included those who traveled, the minutes, who prayed, who spoke, what the message was, and the response from the audience. That information was very important to the future of the ministry. We were in the first quarter of the program, so I had to know its progress, good or bad, to know whether to continue. So far, I was pleased with the way it was coming along.

"You busy, Pastor?" Vaughn Powers peeked his head in after a brief knock at the door.

"Nothing that can't wait; what's on your mind, Brother Powers?"

"I'd like to bring something to your attention, and maybe we can bring it to the table in our next board meeting."

"What you got?"

"Well, a few of the guys around here were interested in getting a basketball team together, to play other churches in the area; maybe we can take our show on the road?" I had to chuckle a little at Vaughn's excitement.

"Can you play?" I asked out of curiosity.

"Man, you know it! I don't know about the other guys

and how they play under the whistle, but I've been balling since junior high school."

He did have a little height on him, so it was possible that he could have skills.

"Ok, we'll discuss it."

"Thanks, Pastor." He got up to leave when I paused him.

"Hey Brother, do you know anything about why there's a trash bag over my parking sign?"

"Oh, I thought someone alerted you. We had a bit of vandalism early this morning. It turns out, someone spray painted a racial slur across your sign."

"Was mine the only one that was hit?"

"Yes, sir. We don't know why they targeted only you."

"It's okay. I'll have a look at it. I'll also review the surveillance cameras to see if I can make out who the assailant was."

"Alright, well if there isn't anything else, I'm going to prepare for prison service coming up."

"Oh yeah, how's that going?"

"Very well, actually. The guys over there have really been enjoying us and we've had fun with them as well. Honestly, I didn't really think it would be like that."

"Like what?"

"You hear all these stories about prisons and the hard core inmates that fill those places. After hearing some of the testimonies from a few of the guys, I realized that they aren't too different from you and me."

"They are different, though. They've committed heinous crimes; some of them anyway."

"There's a side to them that you don't know; it's an experience that can't be explained. Once we bring forth the spirit, the environment seems to make everyone equal. No sin is greater in the eyes of God. Whether it's a speeding ticket or robbery, God shows no partiality."

"Speaking of speeding tickets, you know that ticket you got coming back from Lofton will be handled by you personally." He stood there with his mouth wide open. He obviously was trying to keep that little episode a secret.

"Vaughn, there are a lot of things that I'm aware of. It's up to you whether you are responsible. And before you let the thought cross your mind, The First Lady did not inform me of this. Little do you guys know, she doesn't jump at the chance to run and report things to me just because she is my wife. That's not her style. Just so you understand, I know because I need to know. It's my job to keep things decent and in order."

"I totally understand, and I'll take care of that ticket pronto."

"I'm sure you will. Have a good evening, Brother Powers."

"You too, Pastor."

Mrs. Chambers came in just as Brother Powers was leaving.

"Are you ready for your appointment, Pastor? He has

been waiting in the vestibule for quite some time. Evidently, it must be important."

"Well, by all means, send him in."

A few moments later, a tall figure sauntered through the threshold to my office. My eyes took his in and got stuck there for some seconds. Silence filled the room as the space between us dissipated. He approached my desk, glancing at the certificates and awards that adorned the wall behind me. He then drew his attention to the framed pictures on my desk, a couple with my girls, and one or two with Sandra and I, back when she was smiling brightly, happy to be The First Lady. That was the one he chose to pick up and inspect. He placed it down and then took a seat.

"Why am I not surprised that you are here to see me?"

CHAPTER FIVE

COOKIE

A butterfly is what he called me. As I recalled the phone conversation Adrian and I had, that simple compliment resonated in my thoughts and remained with me throughout the week. We were approaching the weekend, which was when we traveled to Lofton State facility to have our service. I couldn't help but think about how excited the guys are to see us when they come through the door to the multipurpose room. It lets us know that what we're doing is having an impact.

On our trip down the road, my mind drifted to our late night talks. I knew it wasn't proper for a woman in my position to entertain conversations of that nature with a man outside my marriage, but it was so free and refreshing. He really spent a lot of the time listening while I talked. I mainly vented about situations that I was going through, things that I'd tried to discuss with Carl, but he had no interest in hearing me. Adrian was very objective and gave good advice when asked; right now, that was a perfect remedy for my wounded heart.

I found it amazing how someone who had only known me a few months understood me better than the man I'd been sleeping next to for almost two decades. I mean, it wasn't like I didn't try to bring things to Carl's attention; he just got so consumed with the church and all of his duties as the Pastor that, to me, this seemed less important. Lately, there had been more stressful times than good times around our home. Ultimately, my happiness had to matter, too. The only peace I experienced was the time I spent with Reecie. She loved me without conditions; I wish I could say the same about Carl.

Happiness is what I'm searching for and, for the time being, talks with Adrian makes me happy. Such a contrast from what I experience with Carl, we spend so much time arguing and disagreeing that the anticipation of a conversation brings me stress. I know I'm supposed to feel bad, but I don't. Every attempt I made to make a reconciliation, Carl thwarted by denying we had problems. That became a tiresome battle, one that I didn't see myself winning.

The years are passing by like sports cars on an empty expressway. Meanwhile, I'm in the slow lane, hoping my vehicle will make it. Just like a reliable car, we require maintenance; as a woman, I require maintenance. I can't remember the last time Carl and I were intimate. It seems like the passion has seeped out like a slow leak in a balloon. Actually, we're more like a porcelain vase; cracked in a few places, but put back together. We appear fixed to the naked eye; however you add a little water, and there are leaks everywhere.

Right now, I'm embracing self-gratification. Every day, I try to find something to believe in, some sort of hope to get me through to tomorrow. My ministry, my daughter, and my newfound friendship with Adrian are what fills my time these days.

"Sister Andrews, are you going with us?" Sister Matthews interrupted my thoughts; almost embarrassing how I drifted off like that.

"Uh...okay...hey; yes, I'm here with you," I said, trying to recover.

"We're getting ready to pray, wanted to know if you would lead us." I hadn't even realized we entered the prison grounds.

"Sure. Let's bow our heads. Father God, allow the spirit to move in this place. Let your word flow through us and edify these young men of faith. You are the Most High God, and there is power in your name. We are thankful to be used to bring you glory. These men need a word; they need deliverance, healing, restoration, but most of all, they need to see your magnificence in us. We are proud to be vessels for you. We are willing messengers doing your will. In the mighty name of Jesus we pray, Amen!" A chorus of *amens* filled the van just as we parked.

Prison officials greeted us at the first post and led us through the security procedure. It seemed to get easier each time we came; I guess they're getting more familiar with our group. It's funny; I remember how frightened and unsure I was the first time we came up here. Now, I was more comfortable with the procedure. Even Sister Matthews didn't get upset when they pulled her in a side room to check her. The wire in her bra always set the metal detector off. It wasn't her fault she has breasts for days; she'd been busty for as long as I'd known her, and it hadn't been an issue until now. I guess they didn't want her smuggling anything in. I'd seen her bra; she could fit a small child in there!

Inside the multipurpose area, the usual chaplain aides were present to assist us with the setup. The music equipment was already in place when the inmate choir began filing in. To me, they were the highlight of the trip. I enjoyed hearing them sing. They had incredible harmony and moved with precision, which was proof that they practiced hard. We joined in on a couple of songs, really ushering in the spirit.

I really missed a note when he walked into the room from a side door. Luckily, the song was closing. I watched as he took a seat on the front row until we finished.

"What are you doing here so early?" I asked as Adrian approached. There was no security on post yet, so the atmosphere was a bit more relaxed. I was still mindful of my movement, just as was he. We could never be too careful because as he told me on the phone, there was always someone watching. I could hardly contain my smile when he began to speak.

"I work in the counseling area." He pointed to the door he had just come from. "Tonight is my late night, so I had to help with the equipment. I'm responsible for securing everything after you guys leave."

"Oh," was all I could muster up to say.

"Yeah. Normally, I'd be trying to find a way out of it, but I remembered that you guys were coming so I agreed. I had to play it like I was upset but, on the inside, I was anxious to greet you guys."

"You want to meet them?"

"Sure. Your church is so powerful, I'd be honored."

I led Adrian around and introduced him to the church family. He seemed excited to meet everyone, and my crew extended pleasant greetings to him as well. He paused to have a brief conversation with Brother Powers. Sister Allen pulled me aside to whisper something to me.

"You know, I've never seen you with such a glow," she remarked.

"What are you talking about?" I said, trying to mask my expression. I guess I failed in my attempt; she read right through it.

"Look at you, you're blushing now!" She pushed me playfully. "It's okay, he is handsome and I, for one, don't blame you. Love comes in different packages; big, small, short, tall, and even free or locked up. It's all about where you find happiness."

"Who said anything about love?"

"You don't have to speak it to show it."

"For the first time in a while, I have discovered happiness. A conversation so free flowing is hard to find."

"Well, it turns out I'm the keeper of your secrets."

"Girl, you're a soldier. I thank you for being the friend I need. My husband hasn't questioned you about that money, has he?" I was sure he'd be on to the missing funds I had used to bond Maxine out of jail.

"He was definitely suspicious of something wrong in the treasury department but, like I told you, I'm good at what I do."

"I'll just trust you on that."

As we were speaking, the crowd began filling the seats. Adrian took a place next to a guy wearing an apron; I guess he was on the cleanup crew with him. We caught eyes a couple of times while the choir ushered in the spirit through a rendition of "Jesus is Real!" Brother Powers stood at the podium as the song was ending. He waited patiently for the crowd's restlessness to subside, then raised his hands to the heavens before he addressed them.

"Hallellllujah! Praises to the Most High!" Everyone rose to their feet again and began clapping and stomping their feet in unison. That brought a smile to his face, and mine too. It made me feel good to see these guys submit themselves to the spirit.

"Alright, alright, you may take your seats, gentlemen. Did you feel that? That's what it means when it says in the word, 'When two or three are in the midst, the Lord is present there also.' We are responsible. It is our faith, our belief, our relationship that draws the spirit near. The Holy Spirit is a helpmate, given to us as a gift, something in the meantime to hold us down until Jesus comes for us.

"Let's talk a little about the power of the spirit and how it works in our lives. When the word speaks of that still, small voice, it's referring to the Lord working through the spirit. It's like when you have to make a crucial decision and your conscience is leading you in one direction or another, the spirit will show you the right way to go. All you have to do is tap into it. Prayer builds the relationship and allows God to get personal with you; the spirit is His way to guide you in your life."

Brother Powers had everyone's attention this evening. His message was a little different than his last delivery. It was more of a lesson, and they really had to listen to get the full effect. He referenced scripture to back up his teachings. Once they left, they would definitely be full of spiritual food.

We closed with a strong prayer, then dismissed. The security working the service was expeditiously trying to usher us out. I tried my best to get with Adrian once more, but all we could do was make eye contact. It was probably best; I didn't want to put him in a bad position with them.

After all, he had to reside there and I'd feel awful if he got into trouble because of me.

On the way back, I sat in peace, looking at the steady downpour that accompanied us on the busy expressway. Watching the rain symbolized a cleansing; not only of the earth, but what I felt I needed to take place in my life. Rain was also God's way of saturating and preparing for growth. In His sight, each drop had an intended purpose. It was truly amazing how we viewed rainfall as natural. God made his supernatural intentions.

I pulled out my cell and dialed Maxine's number. She has been the one I can confide in about almost anything. Sharing today's joy with her would be no different. Max didn't judge, she didn't criticize; she wasn't even opinionated unless I asked, and I love her for that.

"Hey Cookie, what's going on?"

"On the road. We're coming back from our visit to the prison."

"Oh yeah? How's that going?"

"Very well. I think we're making great strides with the guys. With each trip, a few more men come forward and confess, then commit to changing their lives. It's a blessing to see the transformation."

"That's good to hear. Personally, I'd be a little apprehensive about going into a prison and interacting with murderers and rapists."

"When we go in, we don't see them as that. They're actually respectful, clean-cut, sharply dressed men in there. A few are very nice-looking. Trust me, Max; you'd be surprised by what you saw."

"Humph...sounds to me like you've seen a lot."

"You ever heard the saying, *The good men are either married or locked up?*"

"Now that's funny, because some of the girls over at the salon where I get my hair done were having an open discussion about that topic. I just listened as they went back and forth on the subject. One older woman explained that because there were so many men expressing their homosexuality in the city, she would rather share a man than take a chance with a man who appears straight but is actually gay. That's how she justified dealing with a married man."

"Wow, that's deep."

"Another woman explained how happy she was in her relationship. She said even though there was an age difference, it was far more fulfilling to be in love than to worry about the acceptance of others. When she flashed her sparkling engagement ring, her smile was wide and bright when she declared that her fiancée had just been released from prison after serving ten years. Her motto was *good things come to those who wait.*"

As I rode listening to Max recount those stories, it made me think about myself and, even more importantly, my happiness. I had to make some critical decisions, and soon.

"Max, when can we schedule a session?"

"I'm good Monday through Wednesday, just pick a day."

"Okay, I'll let you know before the weekend's over."

"Sounds good."

Right as I ended the call with Max, a text came through:

I enjoyed seeing you, and I want to see you again and again and again.

I knew exactly who it was from, and it made me smile.

CHAPTER SIX

Adrian

Seeing Cookie the other night was bittersweet. On the other hand, interacting with her for that brief time made me feel alive, almost like I wasn't locked up. We talked freely about a few things. I got a chance to meet her church members and I even took in her scent, which sent me into a daze.

Now, what I didn't like was the feeling of helplessness I had when Officer Adkins ushered them out like they were on fire or something. He was always doing the extra, just to impress his superiors. They weren't even around and he was showing out. I saw the look in her eyes as she tried desperately to weave through the crowd to get to me.

Then I saw her body language slump in submission to the authorities. She probably knew that any attempt to come my way in resistance would cause trouble for me.

I cursed Officer Adkins silently for acting the way he did. He wasn't always like that. It wasn't until he was passed up for sergeant twice that he started to change for the worse. He went from joking and playing with inmates to locking them in the hole for simple infractions. That created enemies for him which, in this environment, was not good. Once we saw him transform, we did our best to stay out of his way. One thing about prison, if you did someone wrong unjustified, the karma would hit you square in the ass and, a lot of times, we got a chance to witness it.

So, although I was angry with Officer Adkins, I realized that his actions had consequences. If I would've reacted to how he handled the church group, then I too would've had to deal with my own consequences. Instead, I was grateful for being able to see her, even touch her. All of my senses got an opportunity to experience her. Like Brother Powers explained, Paul, who went through extreme circumstances, was thankful for the little things. If we all took that same approach, we'd have a much more valuable life.

Work today was a bit harder than usual; my head was still in the clouds from the service the other night. The message was fitting, the fellowship was necessary, and the presence of the lovely Cookie made me appreciate God for sending this angel to greet me. All in all, it was a great escape from my hectic life.

My day on detail was supposed to be my solace away from the dorm. For some reason, I couldn't seem to get into my groove. I cleaned all the offices, filed papers for the counselors, ran some errands, took out trash, and laid down wax in silence, trying to get my head together. Keeping busy always helped me with my thinking process; problem was, people tended to perceive silence as attitude. Pam was one of the first ones to notice.

"Adrian, you haven't said a word all day. Did I do something to you?"

"No, not at all.".

"Well, then, what's wrong?" Her expression showed deep concern.

"Just been absorbing a lot in the past few days. Doing time, you're gonna have ups and downs."

"I surely can understand that but you have always kept the same temperament since you have been up here. So when you change, I notice."

"That's nice to know that you're taking notice of me." She gave me an incredulous look.

"What's that supposed to mean?"

"Nothing."

"Adrian, don't give me that. I know you better than that."

"Really? If you knew me like you say then you'd be in my corner." She was absolutely astonished by what I said. Our voices were escalating as if we weren't standing in her office, it was more like we were having this discussion on neutral turf outside of the prison.

"I can't believe you feel that way. Adrian, I thought I've shown you just how much I'm on your side."

"How? By doing what?" Her eyes sank to avoid looking at me. She really didn't have an answer because all we've done is flirt and have sex. Sure, it's fed my carnal appetite but I'm seeking substance. I'm actually looking for a rider, someone to help me in the fight.

"Pam, I'm trying to get free and it doesn't seem like you're on that plan."

"I am!" She cried out.

"Shhh....Pam, there are other counselors still here."I had to calm her emotions, any recklessness could've gotten us both busted. That's where responsible driving came in, someone had to see the road clearly before the everyone in the car suffers. I was just revealing the truth but part of me was feeling the after effects from seeing and speaking with Cookie. My irritation with Pam was evidence of the effect Cookie had on me. It was obvious that our connection was my stronger than the one Pam and I shared. I didn't feel a twinge of guilt either.

"Adrian, what more is there for me to do? Just tell me," she whined out.

"When I figure it out, I'll let you know" Truthfully, things were changing inside of me, that wasn't something that could be explained to her. It wasn't her fault canoer woman had my heart.

CHAPTER SEVEN

Carl

When I look at myself in the mirror, I see a man who's trying to be the best Pastor, father, and husband a man can be. That's the order of priority I've tried to live my life for most of my married years. It's taken me a while to find my place in this world, and then God revealed my purpose. Help those who can't help themselves, help them find their way.

So when my reflection looks back at me and asks the question, *"What's happened to your family?"* I can't seem to come up with an answer. My pessimistic mindset tells me that things will get worse before it gets better. I try to stay positive, but if I'm judging the current state of my marriage, we have an uphill battle to recover our family unity.

Hopefully this church revival will bring us closer.

They're presenting our church with a humanitarian award as well as a ceremony, so that's definitely something to celebrate. Sandra should be proud of the work she's done in the choir as well as with the prison ministry. I know she was reluctant at first, but she has really warmed up to the task, taking on leadership responsibilities with the group. My plan is to extend our services to other facilities around the state. That way the state will provide more funding which will certainly help the church's finances.

Speaking of finances, I've been meaning to schedule a meeting with Sister Allen regarding an accounting issue that keeps surfacing. I had my personal accountant come in and check the log from last quarter's expenditures. I've been working with Sister Allen for years, and for me, she's part of our family, but the inconsistencies could not be overlooked. I trust her, but trust only goes so far, this is business, nothing personal. Once I pinpoint where the error is, and who is responsible, I can rest a little easier.

As First Lady, I wish Sandra would be a bit more involved in our church issues. That's where a lot of our arguments stemmed from. When she questioned my commitment at home assisting with the parenting, I came back with questions about her involvement in the church activities. At least she should show support to groups that she previously had a part in. Our union started in the church; now it seemed like she was drifting spiritually.

I certainly notice that she's drifting emotionally. The intimacy in our home is nonexistent. The bedroom is as cold as winter in the Upper Peninsula, and I don't see signs of thawing out any time soon. When I talk to other married men, theirs don't sound like mine, so I wonder what makes us so different. What is it that I've done to push her away? Maybe I should put up more of an effort to show her affection and just how much it's needed in return. I don't want it to seem forced, ideally, I would love for her to step into the room in something sexy, and then engage in a sensual encounter with her deprived husband. But in my world, that just sounds like fantasy.

This revival weekend should have everyone in better spirits; it's always helped us as a family in the past. Sure the kids have grown some, and Sandra and I have gotten older, but I still have hope and as the word says.....""And hope doesn't disappoint us." Better spirits means a better chance of changing with our intimacy, Lord knows I need it.

"Hey, Carl! You gonna let me get in there? You spend more time grooming than a woman does," Sandra snapped through the door. She was so over dramatic.

"I'm coming out now," I answered ignoring her degrading comparison to a woman's primping. When I opened the door, she had her towel tied loosely around her torso, her hair down across her shoulders. Sandra's skin looked soft softly moisturized and had the scent of the Dove soap she had showered in.

"All I have to do is my hair, Carl, I won't be long." She shifted to get by me and with her sudden movement her towel undid itself falling to the floor. My wife's naked flesh was fully exposed to me and I felt like some kind of a stranger looking at her with wide open eyes. Nice firm breasts with caramel brown nipples seemed foreign to me even though they belong to a woman I've been with for nearly fifteen years.

My erection was instant and evident by the protrusion in my slacks. As if she felt violated, she instantly covered her private areas, and then scurried past me into the bathroom. I was left there harboring mixed emotions. Part of me was aroused beyond belief by seeing my wife's body, yet embarrassment rested upon me when she looked at me like a stranger. It was as if I was watching her through a window, like a Peeping Tom getting caught gazing. I felt so detached at that moment.

My cellphone's ringtone broke me from my mood. Following the melody, I found it in my suit jacket pocket.

"Hey, what's up?" I answered on the fourth ring.

"So that's how you greet an old friend? I'd hate to see how you treat an enemy."

"It's just been a difficult day, don't take it personal."

"I'll try not to. Why are you talking so low I can barely hear you." I don't know why I began the conversation in the room.

"Because she's in the bathroom." I whispered.

"I figured as much. So when are we finally going to get together?" I exited the room to find some privacy.

"Don't really know, things are always difficult. I've

been patient but limited communication wasn't what I anticipated when we first met. We agreed to a friendship."

Yes, we did, but you also knew my position and situation. I was very clear from the beginning. Now that you're caught up in your feelings I'm supposed to change how I operate?" I heard some stirring in the bedroom. The voice on the other end began getting irate, when the volume raised, the bedroom door opened. I pressed the END button just as she looked up at me. Walking out she looked stunning, hair styled immaculately in an up-do with curls spiraling down the side of her face.

"You look absolutely beautiful, "I complimented. Her lips parted to respond then the melody chimed out and Sandra's whole expression changed.

"You want to get that, seems like someone really wants to talk to you." She brushed past and went down the stairs. I ignored the call, watching the call go to voicemail.

The revival started in grand fashion. The choir and dance team performed, filled with the anointing bestowed upon them. The Holy Spirit was definitely in the building. Song after song seemed to lift the congregation higher and higher. The crowd was unbelievable, reaching record numbers in attendance. Our open invitations to non-members who shared in our joy in worshipping the Lord seemed to have an incredible response.

Brother Powers led with opening prayer, and then fell into the message. Everyone enjoyed the young minister's engaging way of delivering the word. He had the teaching style of a Charles Stanley, the story-telling style of Joel Olsten, and the hair-raising spirit-moving impact of a T.D. Jakes. All of these qualities in a youth minister are rare and we are blessed to have him on our team.

As he closed his message, the crowd was on their feet shouting, jumping and praising. It took some time for me to bring the noise level down to speak.

"Thank you Brother Powers, thank you," I applauded along with them. "He is truly powerful! A name befitting a great man of God. This is a wonderful occasion and I see a lot of new faces out there. Some of you have never been in an atmosphere like this, and we are enthused to have you here with us. Our family opens its doors to you, and right now I'd like to welcome anyone who wishes to open their hearts to us." There was some shifting and stirring about in the congregation.

"C'mon, don't be bashful, anyone is welcome." A woman made her way through the crowded pew into the aisle. She hobbled a bit like she was suffering from a bad hip. Immediately, I felt like she needed healing. As she approached, I could see the weariness in her face; something she was experiencing was aging her before her time. Struggling to climb the three steps to the podium, she gave me a half grin when I handed her the mic.

"Hello, my name is Myriam," she said in a labored voice. "I just want to thank you, Pastor for opening your doors to us." I thanked her for her sentiments, and then told her to take her time. It appeared that she had something heavy on her mind. "My twenty-three-year-old son was killed last week. He was doing all the right things, recently graduated from the University of Maryland with a Bachelor's Degree in Criminal Justice. He had dreams of becoming a police officer. He never had as much as a speeding ticket, so that night when he was stopped and questioned about a broken tail light, it didn't cross his mind that his life was in danger." The whole church was in complete silence as she spoke from her heart.

"It's okay, Sister," I encouraged. I looked down at my wife for reassurance, but the blank stare gave me an unsure feeling about where our connection was. We used to be able to speak to each other without words, which was a while ago. Now our body language speaks of war and pain; uncertainty and distance; alienation and rejection. Hearing this woman's wounded spirit made me question the world. She began to break down.

"When I answered the door and the police officer began to tell me what happened to my baby, my only child, I could already sense what he was attempting to say. It was the details that changed my sorrow to anger. How nonchalant he described the incident made me despise his visit. He said when my son tried to explain that he was aware of the broken tail light and had already purchased the replacement; he moved to show him the receipt and the officer on duty fired into the vehicle on impulse. His explanation was that he saw what appeared to be a weapon on the center console of the vehicle. It was a taser, something he felt he needed to ward off potential robbers. He didn't want to carry a gun until he went to the police academy and graduated, that way he could be properly trained." Looking out in the congregation, men and women were wiping away tears.

"This is our community and I think it's just so sad to see our police officers misusing their power. The same people my son tried desperately to become like were the ones who took his life. How's that for irony? Today I'm asking for your prayers, not only for me and my family but also for a community of young people who are dying before they have a chance to experience life. Pastor, this place here seems like a haven of hope, and I'd be honored to join, becoming a member of your family."

"Ms. Myriam, " I said, taking the mic from her willing hand, "I think we'd be just as honored to have you as a part of us. We could learn a whole lot from you. Your spirit is infectious, and support is what you would receive from us at Victory in Faith." As she started her descent from the stage, a uniformed man made his way to the aisle and down to meet her. He was a police officer from Prince George's County, well built, appearing to be in his early thirties. Myriam's eyes didn't seem to see him until he was upon her. She raised her head and met his gaze. Looking him up and down, the uniform instantly triggered her emotions. She lifted her hand to slap him across the face, the man stood boldly, didn't flinch. Then, as if a healing spirit came over her, she fell into his chest, into his strong embrace. They stayed there for what seemed like minutes until he walked her to an open seat and sat with her.

"That's the power of healing! That's the power of the Holy Spirit!" The congregation roared in agreement. "Is there anyone else who feels moved to come forward?" When I saw who entered the aisle, I regretted asking the question. He walked towards me confidently, eyes fixed on me and me alone. All I could hope for was that he wouldn't make a scene. That was the last thing that I needed in front of my people, and especially my family. Not today.

CHAPTER EIGHT

COOKIE

Carl must think I'm the biggest fool walking the Earth. He may have the wool over the church's eyes but not me. I nearly heard his whole conversation the night of the revival. I was in the bathroom composing myself after that uncomfortable experience with Carl seeing me exposed. I know it sounds strange that a wife would feel uncomfortable in front of her husband, but we're just not in that same space. I got out of his view as quickly as I could.

What Carl doesn't know is that his voice carries even when he thinks he's whispering. Whomever he had on the phone had his undivided attention and he didn't realize I was listening. Funny thing about it is when we got ready to go he gave me a halfhearted compliment which was just a cover for his phone ringing in his pocket. I walked past him as if I didn't hear him or that phone.

The revival produced some mixed feelings for me. It really made me think about the serious problems in the world and especially in our community. That was a very touching moment between the police officer and Ms. Myriam. I feel so bad for her, my thoughts were with my daughters in that moment, wondering if I'd be that strong if my worlds turned upside down. I'm more concerned about Chloe than Reecie right now. She has the potential to be a good kid, but it's the outside influences that pose a problem. With college quickly approaching, my hopes are that she welcomes a new group of friends, ones that will steer her in the right direction.

Gabriel seems to have a hold on Chloe, and the element he comes from will certainly put her in danger if she's not careful. We can only watch her for so long and Carl acts as if nothing is wrong with their relationship. As a father, he should be more alert to the warning signs. Now I didn't tell him or Chloe how he kidnapped me for a few hours, but I believe that was a warning sign, enough for me to try to persuade her to leave him alone. Problem with that is our relationship is already on a soft foundation, so pushing her too hard will push her right into his arms.

I really needed some friendly advice so I invited Max out to lunch at one of my favorite eateries, Chamber's Loft, a spot in Silver Spring with great guacamole dip.

"Hey girl, I'm so glad you called me, the patient I was just with was working me overtime, because of my privacy clause I can't detail our session but know that after while I'm going to need therapy myself," she joked breaking the ice.

"I get it. Everybody needs somebody to vent to, that's why I confide in you."

"Well thank you, Cookie. So what do you have going on in your world?"

"Where do I begin? Besides my marital issues which you know about, and the situation with my daughter's boyfriend, I'm managing life pretty well." I answered sarcastically. "Actually, Max, I feel like I'm losing it over here. I don't know what I feel about Carl anymore. We barely speak, and when we do it's so cold, you can tell there's tension in the air. The intimacy is nearly gone. The other day, I was heading into the bathroom and accidentally dropped my towel in front of him.

"Oh really? What happened?"

"Nothing. That's what I'm talking about. No arousal on my part. He caught an erection but it didn't affect me in any way, in fact, it was almost a turn off."

"Wow! Are you feeling okay?"

"Yes, I'm fine, why do you ask?"

"Because it usually takes a lot for a wife to not be sexually attracted to her husband. When the intimacy is gone, the love is not too far behind.

"Now I do love Carl for the life he has provided for me and the kids. As a father he has done an admirable job, not outstanding, but admirable. To say that sparks are flying, that would be farther from the truth."

"I have counseled a few couples with situations like yours. They never end well. To be honest, I don't even know what advice to give you because it sounds to me like most of the damage has been done before we ever started meeting."

"These problems have existed for too many years for me to remember. The fact that he turned down my attempts at counseling was a sign that the marriage was failing."

"That's a shame, Cookie; you deserve to be happy in your life. When two people take vows it's supposed to be for better or for worse."

"It's hard for me to pick out the better days, so many bad ones have overshadowed." My tone was somber and I felt like I was bringing the mood down on our peaceful lunch date. "Enough about my issues, what's going on with you? Any word from your lawyer?"

"I had to bring on some additional help; they're preparing a defense for me now. Just the fact that I have to go through this is mind boggling. I shouldn't be worrying whether I'm going to jail or being watched because I may flee before my court date. For most people, those thoughts don't even exist."

"I know, Max, you definitely don't deserve this madness."

"Speaking of madness, I'm still concerned about those

things. They probably know by now that I'm out on bond, and who knows what type of eyes they have on me. I'm quite sure they haven't forgotten about the money they gave me to change my story."

"But you did what they asked, and it got you jail time. How were you supposed to know the judge wasn't going to buy it? Sounds like a no win situation. What do you think they're going to do?"

"Honestly, I don't have a clue. I mean, even if I get the money back to them, who's to say that they still won't kill me for not helping them or for fear I may tell the cops what I know."

"You wouldn't do that would you? Not really a safe move."

"Of course not. I'm not trying to dig a deeper hole than I'm already in."

"What do you really know about the guys who gave you that hush money?"

"Not much, why?"

"How much is not much?"

"Well, they're into drugs, guns, and money, you know, typical street dudes. The kind you want to stay away from. Why? What you thinking about? I see your wheels turning."

"We need to find a way to get next to them." Her eyes nearly popped out of her head.

"Didn't you just hear me say these guys should be

avoided at all costs? Now you're trying to do a meet and greet? Cookie, we're not street folks."

"Max, I wasn't always in the church. I still know some people who travel in those circles. It's just a matter of locating them, finding where they hang. Everybody has a pattern of behavior, it's human nature." I know she thought I was crazy, but we had to get her out of this jam, and the only way was to fight fire with fire. "If you can think of anything, let me know."

"Oh....ok, I hope you know what you're doing."

"Trust me, Max."

On the way home from my lunch date with Maxine, thoughts swirled in my head about what I could to help out. Her situation was very tricky and the only way out that I saw was to eliminate her adversaries, but how? There had to be some information on those guys that Max is not disclosing. I stopped at a stop light, letting my thoughts settle. A dark, tinted SUV pulled up next to me. It sort of reminded me of the one that stopped to meet Max that day to give her that envelope. One thing about my memory, it focuses in on details. This particular vehicle had some chips in the paint near the gas tank, and some very noticeable blemishes on a truck that clean. The same thoughts I had that day needed to be confirmed. I wanted to know if my hunch was correct, so I dialed Max.

"Hey." I greeted cautiously, not wanting to alarm her. The truck moved into traffic. I followed slowly.

"What's up, Cookie? Did you forget to tell me something?"

"No, but I was hoping you did. I know this is a long shot, but do you happen to remember what kind of car those guys drove?"

"What? I don't know, some sort of sports utility. I remember that it was black, tint all around."

"There are a lot of vehicles like that, was there anything distinct that you can think about, anything?"

"I've seen it a few times but I didn't really pay attention. Wait, their antenna was bent up a bit and there was some chipped paint around the gas tank which was kind of strange for a truck so nice. Those dudes were supposed to have money to get that stuff fixed."

"Oh, thanks Max," I said hurrying her off the phone. I needed to concentrate on tailing them.

"Hold on, Cookie. What you up to?"

"I'll explain later."

"Chloe, what is it?" I answered sounding irritated. She had been calling back to back ever since I had pulled up to that house.

"It's Dad, he's being unfair." Typical Chloe, every issue with her is over the top. I was trying to stay focused on the house that the black SUV drove to after what seemed like miles of tailing them.

"What's he being unfair about, sweetheart?" I softened my tone to show some concern, especially since it was Carl that was doing the screwing up with her for a change. Usually her issue is with me.

"I asked him if I could go with Gabriel to a basketball tournament in Baltimore."

"A tournament?"

"Yes, it's a day full of games, getting their team ready for the state's championship."

"Let me guess, you'll be gone all day, possibly coming home late in the evening?"

"Well yes, mom, but it's not overnight."

"But you can't figure out why he's tripping?"

"Tripping, mom? Where did you get that from?"

"Listening to you and your sister, anyway, what are you asking, Chloe?" I saw two guys exit the house which caught my attention. Each was carrying a black bag looking around suspiciously. I thought they had seen me but I was parked in a position where it wasn't noticeable.

"Mom.....mom, are you listening to me?" She said interrupting me and my makeshift stakeout.

"Huh, what you say, honey?"

"Dad says he wants you to talk to Gabriel."

"Me? Why me?"

"He spoke with him and told me that he'll make a decision based on what you get from him." Ain't this some mess, we can't even come to a parental decision together.

"So, if I say no after I talk with him, then I'm the bad guy. Now that's not fair to me."

"Please, mom," she pleaded with me. I really needed

to see what those guys were up to. My mission was to find something on them to use to help Max.

"Ok, look give him my number and have him call me this evening, hopefully we can discuss something before I get home."

"Where are you, mom?"

"Out handling some business." I didn't want to get into detail about what I was doing and why I was way out in Seat Pleasant watching some hooligans. She hung up, allowing me to refocus. They took the bags around the side of the house to do something with them. From my vantage point, I could see them dumping the contents into a large heavy duty trash bag. There were stacks of bills bundled by rubber bands tumbling into the bag. I couldn't tell how much but there was definitely a large sum. Two industrial trash receptacles sat beside the house. One of the guys dumped some miscellaneous materials in the other. My guess was that they would come back to get the cash stash in a short while. My wheels began turning at that point.

My phone's ringtone chimed and startled me. It was an unknown number, which I normally don't answer, however, against my better judgment I did anyway.

"Hello, Mrs. Andrews?" A familiar voice asked. We only spoke once before, but I'll never forget his tone, even though it was much less aggressive.

"Yes."

"This is Gabriel, Chloe's friend."

He was much more humble, like he that day was

asking permission to take her to the prom. I know this wasn't that call but that day was coming. He explained to me about the basketball trip to Baltimore and his conversation with Carl. I expressed to him how I felt and how bold he was to even want to ask me anything after the way he treated me, then virtually threatened me if I told Chloe, which I didn't.

The men in the house looked as if they were leaving, which made me spring into action.

"Look, Mrs. Andrews, I know I would owe you big time if you allow me to spend the day with Chloe."

"You're damn right you owe me. So I tell you what, I could use your help with a situation and you could make some money in the process."

"Now you're talking my language. What do you have in mind?"

"I'm out here in Seat Pleasant, on Stanton Road looking into something."

"Stanton Road? That's a dangerous area, what are you doing over there?"

"Long story."

"Don't tell me you're meddling in somebody's business, didn't you learn that lesson already?"

"Are you with me or not? How far are you from here?"

"Shoot, that ain't nowhere from me, maybe ten minutes."

"Well, you need to hurry up."

"What you getting me into?"

"I'll explain when you get here."

I don't think it took him the whole ten minutes when I heard the engine of his Dodge Charger roar down the street. He rolled slowly until he saw the lights flash on my car. He pulled up next to me and let his window down.

"What's up, Mrs. Andrews?"

"Get in."

I explained to him what I saw over at the house across the street. He was all in when I mentioned the money; young guys love the thrill and danger. For me, I'm in it for a good cause.

"So are you sure it's where they left it?"

"Positive. I've been watching the spot the whole time."

"And everybody is gone? Wow, this should be clean and easy."

"Do you have your gun with you?" He paused as if the question caught him off guard. "C'mon, Gabriel, I know you carry. I saw one of your friends hand you a gun after the Roosevelt game."

"Mrs. Andrews, I stay strapped when I'm in the streets, just not around your daughter, "he volunteered.

"Umm huh. Ok, right on the side of the house is the two trash cans. Hit the one on the right, that's where the trash bag of money is."

"Say no more, I'm gone."

He took off across the street, on his way he reached in his back pocket and pulled out what looked like a black mask. He disappeared around the house. After some moments passed I wondered what was taking so long, it was supposed to be in and out. My concerns were increased when I saw the black truck driving slowly up the street in my rear view mirror.

I didn't want to honk the horn to alert Gabriel that would draw too much attention, so I tried texting the number he called me from earlier. As the truck was making its way into the driveway, Gabriel was hot-footing it from the side of the house. He paused when he saw the two men getting out of the truck; this was something he didn't anticipate.

"Hey, what are you doing?" The passenger shouted and pointed to Gabriel, who was still wearing his mask. The question didn't need to be answered, yet he chose to do it quietly with two shots from his 9mm with the silencer attached. The first shot left a hole in the truck's door; the next caught the passenger in the abdomen, sending him falling.

I looked in sheer amazement from across the street, at the events taking place. It was like something out of an action movie, but this was live and in living color. When the driver came around the front of the truck shooting his gun, I started the engine of my car. I knew we would have to make a quick getaway, and I needed to be ready.

Gabriel shot two more times, then made a run for it. Both shots missed its target, one shattering the passenger side window, the other going into the house. With the heavy bag in tow, he zigzagged across the lawn, and then left a hot burning sensation going through his entire left leg. On instinct, he looked back and left two more bullets landing in the chest and shoulder of his pursuant. Gabriel's run turned into a hobble as he made it to his Charger.

"Are you okay?" I yelled out to him.

"I'll be fine, let's get out of here before anyone else shows up. I know a spot we can meet up, follow me."

I could see the trail of blood in the street leading to his car and I wondered if he was truly alright or was he displaying his macho side for me. It made me feel awful that he even got injured getting involved in my madness. Hell, I was involved in this madness for the sake of my friend. As I drove off behind Gabriel, the two bodies squirmed in front of that house, the front door opened and a man stepped out watching us speed off.

CHAPTER NINE

Adrian

Game night. It was football season and sitting in front of the sports television with your meal and favorite drink, placing bets and talking smack was like a high to us. The NFL draws the biggest crowds, those sixteen weeks of intense competition helps us maintain and carry us through our year. Everyone has a team that they root for, since we're located in this region of the country, the Washington Redskins are the hometown favorite. However, tonight's featured game was between the New England Patriots and the division rivals, the Miami Dolphins, squaring off in prime time.

Usually, on these nights, the game is top priority so we tend to get everything out of the way in preparation of kickoff. That means taking showers, cooking meals, and for me, that meant handling my phone responsibilities. By now, most of the dorm knew I had a phone. We were living well in there with probably close to twelve phones in use, so everyone was pretty much satisfied.

I was just wrapping up a call with Pam, making sure that I cleared all the numbers, which was my security procedure. As soon as I pressed the erase button on the last number, that's when I saw them filing in. It was like a sea of black flooding through the front door of the dorm, and the sally port was steadily filling up. When the door burst open everyone was caught off guard.

"Get down! Get down! Everyone on the floor, face down."

From where I was seated on my bed, I could see them, but they couldn't see me yet. There was a little distance between the day room area and the living quarters where I was on my bed peeking through the makeshift privacy curtains I made.

The BOA Squad was who they were, a statewide collection of tactical officers assembled to come into various facilities and totally ransack the institution. Their version of the shakedown was much more severe than any institutional shakedown. This force was much more thorough, and they have zero tolerance for non-compliance, so I've heard from guys who have experienced them. We're getting a full taste of them tonight.

"Bag this contraband up!" One of the commanding officers directed to a couple of his subordinates referring to the collection of soups, coffee, honey-buns, and other miscellaneous items left on the floor under the TV. for gambling purposes. The black suited officers were moving through the day room like a SWAT operation, carrying rifles that shoot bean bag pellets which hurt almost like an actual bullet.

They were heading my way; a few went towards the bathroom and showers area. Guys were being ordered off the toilet and out of the shower naked at gunpoint. They were itching to activate their right to shoot if someone became disobedient.

"Face down on the floor!" They shouted as they moved through the living area. I saw them approaching, I only had seconds to make a decision. Keeping one eye on them, I quickly wrapped the phone up in a spare bed sheet I had then stuffed it down in a bag of dirty laundry I had at the head of my bed. Not a moment later a hand was snatching down my curtain and a gun was pointed at me ordering me down next to my crying bunkmate. He had only been locked up a few months and had never experienced anything of this magnitude. A regulation shakedown was tough for him, this was over the top.

"Everybody up, put your hands behind your back, and walk single file out into the day room!" The boisterous commander barked out. You could hear a pin drop as quiet as it was in there. That was until a young white dude called himself breaking bad with the wrong Squad member. When I crossed the threshold to the day room, I heard a loud smack which could only be skin against skin.

"If I have to tell you to be quiet one more time, I promise you it won't be pretty!" He barked in the boy's reddened face. He got in line without another peep and everyone could tell he was shaken by being slapped in front of everybody in the dorm.

Once we got into tight rows in the day room area, I could see just how many BOA Squad officers were present. There seemed to be close to 150 black suited men waiting for their next orders. They had us so close to each other that you could smell the next man's body odor, because some of them hadn't showered yet.

"Alright men, tear this bitch up!" The commanding officer shouted out. Then they formed groups and filed into the living quarters and began going through all of our property, piece by piece. From my experience, the female officers are far worse during a shakedown than the men. For some reason, they don't leave any stones unturned. That's what had me concerned while I stood there hands clasped behind my back, motionless like a statue.

Out of my peripheral vision I could see the scattered movement going on back there. Our mats were being flipped, clothing sorted, then tossed on the metal bed, and papers were sifted through thoroughly as if they contained top secret documents. This was a true violation of one's privacy, but totally legal according to their standards. At this hour, their assignment was approved by someone much higher than the administration at this facility.

All that was going through my mind was, I hope they

don't find my phone. With these folks, that discovery could result in an instant and prolonged stint in the hole.

"Bed seventeen, step out. Bed thirty-two, step out. Bed thirty-nine, step out. Bed forty-one, step out. My mouth got dry as I tried to swallow. My fear was that the next number they would call would be mine. Everyone that they told to step out was put in handcuffs and escorted out. The way they were ransacking the back, my area in particular, I just knew I was done for.

Moments of silence passed with everyone around me on edge. Once we witnessed J.J., DooWop, Big E, and Syke all to the hole, this situation was getting much more serious than we anticipated. In my mind, I tried to figure out what had brought this on. Whatever it was, these folks were looking deep for something specific.

"Who sleeps in bed fifty-five?" No one answered, but some of the heads turned to look.

"Keep your heads straight!" Look at the back of the man's head in front of you! If you sleep in #55 raise your hand!" The loud voice boomed out.

Ray Crocker slowly raised his hand.

"Please, step out, sir." I couldn't believe my eyes. He spoke to him with such politeness, like Ray wasn't an inmate like the rest of us, he was black too. Two guards walked him out uncuffed. Only a couple of us witnessed the strange act but it was definitely obvious that he was being treated differently.

Almost two hours later, some of the Squad members

made their way from the back area looking weary from the work put in. Trash bags of contraband were carried up to the door to be discarded. After all of them exited the living quarters, one ranking officer spoke orders for us to walk single file back to our beds, still not speaking a word.

I passed by bed after bed looking at the damage. The scene looked like a bombing in Bosnia, property and papers strewn everywhere. When we reached our beds, we were told to remain with our hands clasped behind our heads, quiet until they left the building. Once we heard the front door close, we all took a deep breath, coming to grips with what had just happened.

As people started sorting through the debris left by the whirlwind shakedown, I stood there and just viewed how bad my area was hit. There was no way anyone could survive such a traumatic event without taking a loss of some sort. I just hoped mine wasn't too bad. My first thought was to go to the laundry bag. The way my clothing and paperwork was thrown on the bed, it was hard to tell there anything was.

I tried to organize some of the things on top of my mattress that was flipped back and hanging halfway off the bed. Some of my bunkmate's belongings were on my bed and I assumed I had some of mine on his. When I peeled my mat down, I saw that my laundry bag was sitting on top of my pillow, literally in the same place I had left it. It was as if they were in such a rush to tear up my locker and other personal items, they covered up what I had at the head of my bed. My heart pounded in my chest, not knowing what I'd discover when I went inside that bag.

Even though I wasn't in handcuffs on my way to the hole, I still wanted to make sure I survived and beat the odds. Instead of rummaging through the bag, I just squeezed and gripped through clothing, hoping to feel the contour of my phone. I couldn't believe it! Relief filled my whole body and the tension instantly subsided. It was there.

"Thank God," I said silently. When I opened my eyes, Tree was standing in the cut, mouthing the words *you good?* I just nodded.

The silence among the dorm was broken when Shaka broke out in his lour-accented voice "We've got us a rat in here, they took one out, but there's still another in here!" His comment caused quite a stir. Soon, everyone started shouting out their opinions.

"Yeah, what was up with them taking Ray-Ray out of here?" one spoke.

"You see, they didn't even have him in cuffs," another said.

"I saw that too! Someone else chimed in.

"Why y'all think Ray-Ray is a snitch?" his bunkmate defended.

"Man, look around you! Those folks kicked the door in, tore our shit up, everybody in here took a loss."

"That still don't say he caused this"

"Skooter, wasn't he on your phone at 8 o'clock?"

"I ain't trying to get in that shit, I just lost my joint too."

"I'm just saying, it don't look right."

Tree gave me a look, then leaned down and whispered, "Don't tell anyone that you made it through," and I understood. The tension was too high in the dorm. Everyone was looking for someone to blame for their loss. Everyone was looking for a way to release their anger and even though we've been in this dorm for some time, it doesn't take much to change their mind about you, especially when a loss is involved.

It wasn't until the next afternoon that hostility settled down and all suspicion led to Ray-Ray as the source of the surprise shakedown. At first, it was rumored that he had filed some illegal taxes under various names of the incarcerated, and the paperwork traced back to this prison, names mostly from this dorm. Then when we watched that evening's news, all eyes were glued to the screen when the story ran.

Ray Crocker was one of seven inmates in the state system that the Maryland Department of Corrections was investigating for illegal contraband use in prison facilities. The department enlisted the help of a familiar friend of Ray-Ray, someone he had known for years. This particular female went to great length to contact Ray-Ray. The fact that he had access to a phone and frequented a social network made it easier for him to be located. There's something about the feminine wild that makes it hard for men to resist.

Any available time that Ray had to get on a phone, he made sure that he contacted Sherita, his old friend. They soon became close and spoke of plans for a future after his release. Little did he know, she was baiting him up. Several of their conversations were recorded by her with specific questions being asked to garner the response she needed for her investigation. The last call that was made to her was thirty minutes before the BOA squad came through. It was as if they were waiting for the cue from her to strike and it worked. The squad recovered ten phones from their sting operation, even though the news report stated they picked up a whopping 400 from our location. That was a huge exaggeration, but the numbers made their bust look more impressive.

Sherita's recorded conversation was the missing connection to an ongoing case being built against prison facilities. She did her part by taping her talks with him, then reporting the information to the MDC. It was enough to launch an investigation that triggered this shakedown. The news segment even showed clips of us lined up in the dayroom being shook down.

I finally brought the phone out that evening when I felt the tension was down. Plus, I knew there were guys who needed my help. Losing your lifeline was a hard pill to swallow. And the ones in the dorm who have been with me for a while know my heart. So I took a chance, alerting the dorm that I was willing to let guys contact their families in order to get their money together.

First, I had to let my people know what just took place. Pam was my first call. "Hey baby!" she answered, excited to hear my voice. "I saw the news, was it really that bad? They said they got 400 or 500 phones."

"Not hardly. But we did take a major loss, it was a very tough night."

"I'm sure it was. That guy, Ray Crocker, I think I've seen him in counseling a few times, Ms. Brownlee has him on her caseload."

"Had him, they will probably transfer him after last night's events. He's all over the news now so it will be tough for him to live in peace."

"I'm curious, how did you not lose your phone? I mean, I'm not mad at you, but the images on T.V. looked like they were very thorough."

"Let's just say I had God with me."

"Had to be God, you made it through without a scratch."

"Yes, but it's a difficult position to be in, with everyone else losing."

"You're right Please be careful."

"I will. Let me go, I hear some commotion up by the door."

"Ok, I'll talk to you at work tomorrow."

Nearly everyone in the dorm was crowded at the door. There was someone in the lobby with their property on their shoulder. I couldn't make out who it was with all the people in the way, but it seemed like they were forming a barricade at the door. When I got up there and got a glimpse of who it was they were barring from entering, I couldn't believe my eyes, it was Ray-Ray just getting out of the hole.

The officer was pointing towards our dorm, however everyone in the window was shaking their heads and waving him off. There was obvious hostility, and environment no one would really want to enter into. When Ray-Ray looked at the same faces he had lived with for over a year now look at him differently, he said something to the sergeant on duty, then he escorted him out. We took a stand and would not allow Ray Crocker to put us through another night like we'd just endured. In prison, unity spoke volumes and for the first time in a while, we stuck together and let our voices be heard.

CHAPTER TEN

Carl

"Ok, this has got to stop. Popping up at the revival was dead wrong."

"And how is that, when you gave an open call to the public, well I felt like that applied to me too. You didn't have to hurry me out of there like that. I think that caused more attention than what you were looking for."

"I did what I had to. My gut was telling me that you were aiming to embarrass me in front of my church."

"My church...my church. Is that all you care about?"

"I have other concerns."

"But what makes you happy, Carl?"

That was a loaded question. I said the first thing that came to my mind.

"Serving the Lord, that's what makes me happy."

"If that's the only thing then why do you seem so uptight? And why doesn't your wife share your same joy?"

"Oh Sandra loves the Lord."

"What about her love for you? Do you see that?'

"Why you asking so many questions?"

"Because if you and your wife were in a good space where you shared the same joy and love then we wouldn't be having a thing."

"Is that what we have?"

"I don't know you tell me."

"What I will tell you is my marriage is my business."

"No Carl, actually it has become my business too ever since you invited me in your life. Now you're not gonna shut me out after you got me all into the hopes of us having something."

"Look, I think this was a mistake."

"A mistake? Oh the mistake is trying to stop what you started. You started this, Carl. Why are we discussing this on the phone? Let's meet somewhere and talk."

"I don't think that would be a good idea."

"And why not? You ashamed to be seen in public with me? Or are you worried about your sterling reputation?"

"Ok fine, you want to meet? Let's meet, but understand that this will be it."

"When and where?"

"Lucia's down on 9th street."

"Why down in D.C? Damn pick somewhere in Maryland. Who you hiding from?"

"Fine meet me at the Applebee's in Greenbelt. 7:30."

"7:30, I'll be there."

When I ended the call, I couldn't believe how I had gotten so deep in this situation. Regret washed over me like white water rapids. When I made an emotional decision to get involved, never did I think it would lead to being placed in a compromising position. Now, it was time to end it. I just hoped it didn't come with repercussions.

"Daddy, what does it mean when a boy all of a sudden doesn't call you? Chloe asked, coming into my office and looking distressed.

I didn't know if she caught the tail end of my conversation, but it appeared that whatever was on her mind was important.

"Sweetheart, you never know what could be going on. Try not to read too much into things. It will stress you out. I'm assuming you're talking about this Gabriel fellow."

"Yes. Remember the other day when I asked permission to go to the all-day basketball tournament?"

"Yep, and I told the man that if your mother says yes, then I'll go along with her decision."

"Well, he told her he was going to call her and ask, then I didn't hear from him the rest of that day or the day after the tournament. Do you think he forgot about me and took someone else?" I could tell she was hurt by the tears welling up in her eyes.

"I really don't think that's the case. He wouldn't have gone as far as to ask us to let you go, just to take someone else. It's probably something unexpected that came up, something he needs time to talk about."

"Maybe you're right. It just seems strange, though. This is not like him."

"People change, baby girl, especially at your age. Guys may think they know what they want, but realize that their minds or heart take them in another direction."

She got quiet for a second, I guess to let what I was saying sink in.

"One thing that's for sure is that my love for you will never change."

"I know that, Daddy, but I'm not a little girl anymore. I want to have a family someday."

"And you will in due season. Doesn't mean you have to settle for the first guy who says he loves you. The most important thing is making sure the love you receive is genuine. Your happiness is the key. If that doesn't happen, then the door won't open." She gave me a huge hug, love I haven't felt in a long time in this house.

"Thank you, Daddy."

"You're welcome sweetheart. Where's your sister?"

"I think she went somewhere with mom."

"Ok, I'll speak with her when she gets home. Hey how about we go out and get some ice cream like we used to?"

"I'm not a little girl anymore, Daddy," she whined out.

"You'll always be my little girl!" This made her smile.

"I'll go get my things and be right back."

I had to admit I was feeling pretty good about myself

at the moment. There was a few hours to burn before I had to meet up at Applebee's so spending time with my daughter was right on time. Besides, Sandra was out with Reecie, it was only fitting that Chloe and I be together. This was parenting at its finest. The knock on the door shook me of my parental bliss. I opened it before I took a glance through the peephole and wished I did that first.

"Hello Pop," the voice on the other side of the threshold bellowed out.

"I don't go by Pop," I said sternly.

"Well then what is a son supposed to call his father?" Silence filled the space between us. Truthfully, I really didn't know what to say or how to take this intrusion.

"How did you find me?"

"Is this how you greet your family?"

"I asked you a question."

"Google is a beautiful thing, and the renowned Pastor Carl Andrews is not very hard to find. Now, are you going to invite me in?"

"For what?" I looked over his shoulder and some of our nosey neighbors were goose-rocking out of the windows and doors, wondering who this strange man was at my door.

"So we can talk. You know, catch up on old times."

I looked around, thought about it, then against my better judgment, I let him in. Might have been a mistake, but I was kind of backed against the wall. I turned around and led him to our family living room.

"Nice place you got here, Pop...I mean Dad. Is that what you want me to call you?"

"I haven't decided yet."

"No."

"What are you gonna tell your family about me? It's not like you can deny my existence because here I am," he said with his arms open wide.

"Sit down, son."

"Son, okay now, we're getting somewhere."

"I say that out of respect because you're a young man in my house," he sat respectively.

"So, can we talk?" he figured humility would be a better approach, so he changed his tone.

"Talk about what? You have some nerve coming here."

"I want to talk about establishing a relationship with you. After all these years, I've never had a father in my life."

"You're what, in your thirties? Why now?"

"Damn, Dad."

"Hold on, we don't use profanity in my house!"

"You make it seem like I left you, you left me!" his voice raised and it carried. Chloe made her way to the bottom of the stairs."

"Dad, who is this?" I was afraid of that question, but I knew it was inevitable. I looked at her with uncertainty.

"Chloe, I'll explain later."

"Aren't you going to introduce me to your daughter?"

Now, this was an incredibly awkward moment. Chloe

had begun to walk away before he said that, so her curiosity was sparked. She stood there with her arms crossed, waiting. Carl's presence at this point in my life was a reminder of a dark period that I'd kept suppressed for a long time. His mother and I were in love when we conceived him, but then she started to become unhappy. At first, I thought it was postpartum depression but after a couple of years, I figured it had to be something else. Her actions toward me made me believe that I was causing her discomfort.

At the time, I was working nights as an auditor; this was before my life in the ministry. I came in early one more morning after my shift and was tired, only to find her and my baby boy gone. I tried desperately to find them; however, she made herself impossible to find. It was a nightmare.

For years, I spent sleepless nights trying to figure out what to do. I tried every legal route available to me and still came up empty. Finally, one day, her sister contacted me out of the blue giving me the news that the mother of my child had passed away. My first question was where she left my son. She didn't even know she had a child.

That was a tough pill to swallow; it ripped my world apart. The only recourse I saw was to seek God and his infinite wisdom. My thoughts couldn't develop enough to understand what was happening in my life and pain was way too extreme to handle myself. I needed help from a higher power. I threw myself into the church studying, praying, and ministering hoping to find a way out of the misery that was swallowing me up.

God's answer was to trust in him with all my heart and all my strength, he will direct my path that I had to block out the fact that I had a son somewhere out there. Looking for him was driving me out of my mind. God restored my sanity and I'm eternally grateful. However, the present now stares me in my face.

"Chloe, this is Carl Andrews." It was time for me to stop running from my fears and face the truth.

CHAPTER ELEVEN

COOKIE

"Mom, he still hasn't called me yet and it's been days."

My heart went out to Chloe. It's been a long time since she's reached out to me as a mother. This situation with Gabriel was really affecting her. She would mope around and be real snappy with us, her sister particularly. It wasn't Reecie's fault and she couldn't figure out why Chloe was being so mean.

Truth be told, I couldn't bring myself to tell her what actually happened. I went by the hospital where Gabriel was recovering from his gunshot wound and we both decided that it would be best if he told Chloe. He explained to me how the bullet entered into his thigh from the back and exited through the front just missing a major artery. He shared with me his fear of dying in the same way his favorite player, Sean Taylor did.

Sean was a pro bowl safety for the Washington Redskins. He was trying to protect his family from young robbers and got shot in the leg rupturing a main artery. He eventually died in a Miami Hospital.

Gabriel and I formed a bond. Sitting by his bedside showed me a vulnerable side to this kid. Some days I couldn't believe I was spending time with the same young man who had me tied up in his trunk. Through God I have the power of forgiveness coming to see him was more than his own family has done. My heart wouldn't allow me to let him lay in that bed with no company, especially since I'm responsible for him being there.

Not once did he throw blame in my direction, he said he made his own decision. He was honest in saying that he should have gotten out of there soon, they probably would've missed the men at the house. When he saw how much I broke him off, it seemed to soothe him better than any medication the doctors could prescribe. In total the bag contained $85,000. I gave him $10,000 plus handled all of his medical fees. It didn't seem like much considering how much was taken in, but after I explained why I had to pull the caper, he understood and respected my loyalty to Maxine.

With the remainder of the money I was now able to put the $25,00 back into the church account plus have $50,000 left over for Maxine's situation. As it stands, she's in the red and the money needs to be available in the event she needs it. I do fear that if she pays them goons the money they will kill her anyway because she didn't carry out their agenda. Her paying change negated their plan to have her testimony help Richie Rich's appeal to go out of prison. Now they're back at square one, no further than they were before except $50,000 poorer. That's not going to settle well with them.

We still had to deal with her pending case in court if it's not handled correctly she could go back to jail. That's a bridge we'll have to cross when we get there. For now, I'm going to focus on being the best friend I can be to her. She really doesn't have anyone else in her corner. Besides, friends are hard to come by and I haven't had many lately.

"Chloe, I have a feeling he'll call soon. He's probably going through something serious. He doesn't seem like the type to disappear."

"What's made you a part of the Gabriel Measures fan club all of a sudden? Just a few days ago, you didn't want me spending a day with him, now you're speaking for his character."

"All I'm really getting at is you shouldn't read too much into him not calling you."

"That's the same thing Daddy said." Now, that was a shock. Carl and I actually agreed on parenting tips? What was next?

"Really?"

"Yea, speaking of Daddy, he introduced me to Carl Andrews." I thought my ears were playing tricks on me.

"Who?"

"Carl Andrews. He said he was his son." My heart sunk. What was this girl talking about? Was this one of her games she played to get under my skin?"

"When did this happen?"

"The other day when you and Reecie went to the mall. You guys just missed him because he left right before you came home."

"I saw a silver car driving up the street from this direction."

"I don't know what kind of car he has, but that might have been him."

"Why are you just now telling me? Don't you think that's something I need to know?"

"Daddy told me that he would tell you. He kind of swore me to secrecy." He has seen me every morning since that day, we even met once at the church and he didn't utter a word about having a son. He was in our house, for God's sake.

"That figures."

"Don't bust me out, Mom."

"Oh, I won't. I'll wait patiently for him to have that conversation, then we'll have a real long conversation." Just thinking about it was raising my temperature.

"Max, I couldn't believe it when I heard it myself. Chloe said it so casually."

"Cookie, there's always something going on in your household."

"I know girl, how can you not tell your wife that you

have a son? This happened before us, I hope. I mean from the way Chloe described him, he's a grown man."

"My goodness. Have you talked to Carl?"

"Nope."

"Why not? I'm sure it's eating you up."

"Oh it is, but I'm not gonna give him the satisfaction. Whenever he tells me, I'll be ready to give him a piece of my mind. Until then, I'll act like nothing's wrong."

"That's gonna take some good acting."

"Not really, I've been acting for years; he just don't know it. But never mind about me, what are we gonna do about your situation?"

"I don't know, Cookie, I try not to think about it."

Ah...excuse me, you need to think about it. You got these gangsters out here who are not happy with what happened in court, and by now they probably know that you've made bond."

"You think they know?"

"I'm sure they do. Those type of guys keep their ear to the street, can basically find out whatever they want to know."

"Oh my."

"I'm not trying to spook you, just making sure you aware."

"My focus has been on the case itself and how to keep from doing any jail time."

"What's your lawyer saying?"

"He said we may have to try the fear angle, let the

judge know that they threatened me and that's what caused me to get on the stand and say what they wanted me to say."

"You think the judge will buy it? He was tough on you the first time."

"That's what I'm afraid of. I'm also afraid that those guys are gonna want this money and I don't have it to give."

"How much did you say it was again?"

"Around $50,000."

"Are you sure?" She sounded uncertain all of a sudden.

"Yeah, it was fifty grand. Why?"

"Nothing, just need to know." She looked at me suspiciously.

"Cookie, what are you up to?"

"If I told you, you wouldn't believe it. Just know I got your back."

"Oh, I'll take your word for it. Hope you're not getting yourself in any trouble over me."

"Oh, trust me honey, the trouble is over."

I left Maxine with a bundle of knots in my stomach. I was on my way to see Sister Allen; it was time to settle that debt. She put herself on the line, so I needed to get her off the hook. She told me that Carl had brought in some outside accountants to audit the books once again, he just sensed things weren't right. Even at home, he would mention something about how the accounts were off. I told him he had Sister Allen and she's the best in the business. He would agree and that would be that.

However, that didn't stop his investigation. He looked over his files even called in one of the deacons to double check what he saw. The first thing he reviewed was where the offerings from each Sunday service were stored. For this quarter dollar for dollar was tallied then deposited in the church account at the bank. The figures they had in their system should match ours. Sister Allen made sure the software was updated to reflect any deposits, transfers, or withdrawals.

"Come on in Sister Andrews, he's online right now." She was at her desktop looking at the screen. The intense stare she had told me she was all about business.

"I did what you asked me to do on my way over here."

"Good, good. It should show right here. And there it is. Way to go, Mrs. Brookmire." That's was the older later over at the bank who made the deposit for me. When she saw the stacks of bills I pulled out of the soft sided brief-case. Discretion was of the utmost importance and she handled the situation with care, never letting on her intentions.

"Will he notice the movement?"

"No. See, what he is looking at is a mirage, a temporary glitch. At first, he did see the account was missing the $25,000, but once you made the deposit, Miss Brookmire alerted me, I forged his screen and caused a slight panic for him. Now when he goes back in, he'll see the total as it should be. He'll question himself, probably even call me in there, which I'll act as if everything is normal."

"I'll give it to you, Sister Allen, you're genius!"

"Naw, not me, just made good use of my I.T. degree." We both shared a laugh then got interrupted by a call on her business line.

"Yes Pastor, I'll be right there." She hung up, winked her eye at me, then went to meet with her boss.

Being in control is what Carl thrives on, it's what moves him. So to see him powerless in his own church serves him right. I know what I did wasn't befitting of a First Lady, I do have my faults. All I can do is pray for forgiveness, repent, and move forward in trying to better myself and those around me. Helping Max was something that was on my heart, I didn't really know how I would do it or the outcome. Asking God for his guidance was what gave me peace throughout. Whether right or wrong, I felt like I did what was best for my friend.

CHAPTER TWELVE

Adrian

I see Cookie as a great friend. When she told me about how she helped her girl out and the lengths she went through to make it happen, it gave me a newfound respect for her. We had a wonderful conversation about family and relationships. It was very interesting to hear about her past; I even shared things about myself I'd never shared with anyone.

This prison situation really didn't define me as a person. I actually had a life that was worth being proud of. My past wasn't what had brought me here; my upbringing wasn't filled with hardships and struggles. In fact, my childhood and adolescent years were loving due to my parents doing whatever they had to for their children.

Throughout my school years some of my peers experienced things that never came my way. Our high school had kids that were bused from various areas around the county. Some of these areas weren't in the best condition and the reflection was evident in the way these kids acted. There was a different mentality and it could be seen clearly when these backgrounds were mixed in with the others. This created a cultural melting pot.

Our suburban high school felt the impact of blending students. Antoine Mitchell was one of those students with an extremely bright future both academically and athletically, The teachers and students body loved and respected him and in my eyes, I didn't see him have a single enemy. As an African American student in a multiracial school, he was one that rose above the social issues that plagued these times.

Antoine was a budding track star breaking all kinds of records in Prince George's County. His times were outstanding, good enough to qualify for the upcoming State Championships. There was one more local meet to serve as a tune-up; all the top sprinters were invited, Antoine included. He was a representation of our school, our class, so his success was our success. When the news spread about him crushing the competition, there was cause for celebration.

Some of the guys on the track team decided to throw a pool party at the YMCA in Landover. There were some local boys who made themselves welcome. They were a few years older than the high school age crowd and with them came the presence of liquor. Tension and alcohol was always a bad combination at a party, that's exactly what was brewing that night.

Antoine wasn't much of a socializer, actually he was more on the shy side, attending parties really wasn't his thing. However, he felt an obligation to his team to at least show his face before heading home. He wasn't there a good half an hour before tempers flared between a neighborhood boy and a kid from Bowie over a girl who turned him down.

When the older boy pulled out a gun, it caused pandemonium. He started shooting randomly, hoping to hit his target. People scattered, running everywhere. You could hear the screams from girls echoing off the nearby houses. I had never been in anything like that; fear flowed through me and controlled my movements. All I could do was duck and hide. Most people had that same idea except Antoine. I saw him and a couple others break out into a full sprint. The sudden burst of movement triggered the gunman to shoot sporadically. One bullet caught a girl in the leg and another hit Antoine; he fell to the pavement immediately. After seeing the body fall, the gunman fled the scene.

There were cries and shrieks of anguish when the dust settled and we saw Antoine down shaking, coughing up blood. Someone had their composure and was able to call 911 because I could hear the sirens approaching. By the time the ambulance arrived on the scene, Antoine was semi-conscious. We found out later that he died on his way to the hospital.

Monday came and the whole school was in a funk dealing with the loss of Antoine Mitchell. This was by far our biggest tragedy and for me the hardest thing I had to deal with. I didn't come from an area where guns and violence were prevalent. My parents did a good job of shielding me from that lifestyle. So years later when I got arrested for this crime, I was hardly for the environment I was facing.

"Adrian, I think you are very strong for maintaining and enduring this long."

"I really didn't have a choice."

"Oh yes you did. You could've easily folded up, gave in, and made things easy for yourself."

"That's just it, things would've actually gotten harder."

"Well, I believe in your strength. From what I've heard you have resilience that will only add to your character."

Cookie had a way of building confidence. Our conversations were deep and she kept things lighthearted, very refreshing. Pam and I speak on a different level, our talks are more sensual and flirty. Usually I'll lead then she will follow but with Cookie it's more of a back and forth on all sorts of topics. I can only imagine what a face to face would be like.

"Thanks Cookie, you know how to lift a brother up."

"I've had years of practice trying to lift up a man who was already on a pedestal."

"Marriage takes work."

"I agree, but when it becomes a chore year after year, it's time to reevaluate some things."

"So, am I part of your reevaluation process?"

"You and your questions," she quipped.

"You didn't answer?"

"The time spent with you talking should be your answer."

"Point taken. So, what if I want more?"

"I can give what I have. Right now, it's time. But I admit, I'm enjoying the time. I'd rather spend it all with you."

"You guys are coming Friday, I'm looking forward to seeing you."

"Are you still working on the visitation?"

"Yes, but it's tougher than I thought; not to mention, risky. One to you being a volunteer. I don't want to raise any red flags."

"Makes sense. I'm sure you know what you have to do in there."

"Safety is the number one priority."

"Indeed."

Something was different about tonight's service, I couldn't put my finger on it. When Preacherman stopped by my bunk to see if I was still going, my nerves rose inside. I don't really know why, on nights when Victory in Faith comes to visit I'm usually anxious. One thing was for sure, at least I'd get a chance to see Cookie and that's always a good thing.

I hate to think that the thought of seeing her outweighed the draw to the message, their delivery of the word was very powerful. It's just that I can't deny the attraction between us, if going to church strengthens that then I'm there every time the door opens.

Nothing changed with the movement of the spirit in the room; the praise and worship still served as an usher to us as we entered. It wasn't my night to work late, so I didn't have the luxury of being there early when the guests arrived. Preach and I walked up together, that's when I mentioned to him how I was feeling.

"A.H, what's up?" You've been quiet ever since we left the dorm." Preach knows me better than anyone in our form so he would see any change in my mood and call me on it. We'd been through a lot together over the past year, I consider him my closest friend in here.

"You know when you feel something is off balance on the inside? Can't really put my finger on it, I'm hoping the message will up lift me."

"You know what that's called?" Preacher asked.

"What, bro?"

"A down todder spirit. It's like a long weight coming down on you, but it's invisible."

"Yeah, that's how I'm feeling. How can I get rid of it?"

"This is not a physical thing; you have to pray it off, allow God to do His work."

"That's what I have to work on," I confessed.

"We all do, bro. Trust and have faith; that's the key to peace, happiness, and blessings."

"Amen."

When we entered the sanctuary for the night, there was hardly anywhere to sit. A couple of seats were open close to the front, but they weren't together, at this point we couldn't be choosy. The main thing was that we were in the fellowship of brothers. Around me were some familiar faces, ones who attend church faithfully. I admired their dedication and hoped one day I would be that committed.

Our choir sang a few praise songs then Victory in Faith's choir took over with their melodic hymns. After-wards, they sat down and one of the deacons stood to open up in prayer. I spotted Cookie amongst the others, but did not recognize the newcomer seated next to her. He was brown skinned with a little height on him. He had one of these white collars on so I assumed him to be the pastor... wait could that be The Pastor?

"I'd like to bring to the podium someone who is new to you guys but to us he is revered and noted for delivering a powerful word, our esteemed Pastor Carlton Andrews! Let's give him a warm welcome." We began to applause then everyone joined in. We even rose to our feet to enhance his reception. Cookie and I caught eyes then she averted her attention to her husband. As he spoke, her eyes came back to me, it was a strange transformation. At first I saw love and admiration as she watched him speak then I felt the attraction that we've been sharing when she looked back at me. How was I to read these mixed signals?

I had to admit, he was strong in the word, something that Cookie did mention. His message focused on the fall of man and we have been redeemed through the Lord Jesus Christ through his gospel teachings. I was actually amazed at the depth of his knowledge of the word; it was evident that he had studied for years. It was no wonder how she was taken aback when she first met him.

When she told me how much he had changed throughout their marriage, it was hard for me to picture that man when the man before me was so impressive. It's true that people can have two sides and show you what they want you to see. What's going on in their home has no bearing on what kind of man he is in his church. The church family views him one way, yet his blood family got another version.

My attention diverted back to Cookie. I wondered how she must be feeling inside. After all she revealed to me about the pain and stress she's suffered over the years and to still have to endure the daily rigors of being the First Lady. That little alone carries great responsibility, the mask that she has on right now is just one of the many duties she has to fulfil. My heart went out to her. I gave her a look of reassurance because I could see her hurt inside.

CHAPTER THIRTEEN

Carl

I was almost sure Chloe would tell Sandra that the man who calls himself my son came by the house. After a forced introduction, Chloe's reaction was not what I expected. I thought she would come with a bunch of questions but no, she acted as if it didn't happen. As far as she was concerned, it didn't matter if Barack Obama was sitting in our living room; all she wanted to do was go get ice cream.

Sandra's mood had definitely changed. At first, I figured it was due to a little spat we had regarding the way she was treating the girls. I felt like she was giving Sharice better treatment than she was giving Chloe. Around the house, Chloe was asked to do more chores, and Sandra was constantly on her case about this or that. It seemed like Reecie was exempt from doing certain things, and I didn't think that was right so I spoke on it.

For us, it wasn't nothing new. We bickered over small things all the time, but this sudden change in temperament was due to something else. I noticed her cold nature in our bedroom that spilled over to the church. The day I met with Sister Allen about the accounting issue, Sandra was there in the hallway outside of my office. I saw her, she saw me, but it was like we were complete strangers instead of husband and wife.

She waited there until Sister Allen and I were finished, then she followed her back to her office. The two of them chit-chatted in the can on the way to Lofton like they were best friends, I had never seen them this close. We, on the other hand, had barely spoken three words on the trip. Body language says a lot and the way she was acting her body was speaking volumes.

When we arrived at the prison, she seemed like a whole different person. Her spirit was brighter, she laughed feely and was full of life when she was up on the stage singing. That was the woman I fell in love with, the one whose uncontrollable attraction drew me near. This was something I would need to consult with the Lord about and ask for his guidance because I was at a loss for answers.

As I gave my message, I made a habit of looking at the reaction of those I was trying to reach. I was quite surprised when a couple of times, I caught Sandra in a gaze with one of the inmates in the crowd. The first time, I thought it was just me overreacting but then I saw it again, and once more before I actually closed. At the end of the service, the guys had an opportunity to greet us and let us give an encouraging word. We lined up, and this particular young man was making his way down the line. Hand after hand he shook before he stood in front of me. I looked him in his eyes, then asked this name.

"Adrian Upshaw," he replied confidently.

"Well Adrian, I will pray for you by name."

He moved from me, said a couple things to Brother Powers, then paused at Sandra. That's when my attention focused, and I noticed that same eye contact I saw earlier. I was not mistaken, the look I witnessed was what I used to see given to me. It kind of did something to me, but I held it together all the way back to the church. When I got off the van and made it to my car, I saw that my phone had a few missed calls. I checked my voicemail and was disturbed at the messages I received.

"So, now you're standing people up?" said the angry voice on the recording.

To tell the truth, when my son came through unexpectedly, I completely forgot about my 7:30 meeting at Applebee's. Generally, I didn't make it a practice to stand people up. However, that was an extraordinary circumstance. I was sure I'd hear about it later. The next message spoke:

"This is your mother, Carlton. I don't know what's

going on with you lately, but you need to give me a call. Your brother said something about you need to check your Facebook, someone is putting some untruths on there."

What was she talking about? My brother was always overreacting to things and every time, he got our mother all stirred up. He'd been doing it all our lives. This wasn't anything new.

I remember when I was away at seminary school, he heard from a classmate that I had a verbal dispute with one of my professors. By the time he gave Mom his version of the story, she thought I had got into a physical altercation and got expelled from school. She was so disappointed that I had to get the professor to actually call her and explain the misunderstanding. To this day, she still fell into my brother's foolery.

"I'll look into it, other. So, what else is new? Aren't you having a birthday soon?"

"Yep, sure am." She loved it when people took notice of her. "I'll be fifty-five!" she said excitedly.

"Mother! You will not be fifty-five years old. I hope you're not telling people that."

"Indeed, I do. I don't care if they don't believe me. It makes me feel good to say it." I had to chuckle at her.

"Whatever makes your boat move through the ocean, Mother dear. I have to go. I have a call coming in."

"You youngins always have so much going on. No time to spend with your mother. Cell phones and computers are running the quality of life."

"Now, I have to agree with you on that, mother. I really have to go. I'll call you later."

"Okay baby, until then."

She always ended our calls with that line, and she did it with her attempt at a British accent. Ever since she spent a month in London years ago, she thought she could flow in and out of the dialect at will. I didn't have the heart to tell her it was not working.

I saw the missed call and instantly, a pain formed in my stomach. This was yet another problem I had to deal with. Avoiding the issue would not make it go away. What I was worried about the most was what Sandra was going to say when she found out because eventually, she would and that day would not be pretty. The call started in again. Right now, I wasn't ready to face the music so I pressed IGNORE, sending it to voicemail.

Sandra was in the living room when I came out of my office. She was laughing at something on the television, but when I entered her view, her mood instantly changed. A frown formed on her face and her eyes had a look of disdain. The sad part is I was growing accustomed to it lately. This was the page we were on. I don't know how we got this far gone, but we were here and I have no clue how to fix us.

"So we're really gonna keep doing this? Not speaking? Not looking at each other? Not sleeping together?" I stopped sleeping in our bedroom choosing to rest in our guest bedroom. My statement to her got no response so I tried a different approach, reasoning with her.

"Look Sandra, I know we haven't been on the same page lately but I'm trying here. I'm trying to be a good father, trying to be a good husband, trying to be a good Pastor."

"Humph!" she breathed out. "Seems like the last one is the only thing that concerns you." Finally she speaks and she shoots me that crap?

"I don't understand what you want from me, Sandra. Trying to figure you out is a mystery."

"I'm not sure what I want," she said flatly.

"Well what should I do?"

"Stop trying to figure me out and start trying to figure out what made us a union in the first place because to me that's where the mystery lies." Her words stung like a swarm of hornets.

"What made us a union was your love for me and my love for you."

"Oh give me a break, Carl. Did you really love me or did you love how I would make you look to those precious church members of yours?"

"How could you say that after all these years? You're saying that you've never been happy?"

"Sure I've been happy, but honestly it's been awhile since I've had that feeling."

"I can't believe you could say that."

"It's time, Carl. I just don't quite know what to expect

from you anymore." Her statement was open. I couldn't tell if she knew something or not. She definitely had a poker face on. The doorbell rang which broke our silence. The timing couldn't have been any better.

"Reecie, can you get that sweetheart?"

"Okay, daddy." A few moments later, she came into the living room with a bouquet of roses so big, they hid her face. Who in the world would send flowers here? I knew one thing, they better not be from that boyfriend Chloe'd been going crazy about, especially after the hurt my baby girl had been suffering wondering whether he was going to call or not.

"Who are those from, baby?" Sandra asked in a light tone.

"There's a card in here somewhere, the delivery man said. Wait...here it is. It says:

"Cookie, I wanted to send a token of my appreciation."

Before I knew it, Sandra leaped up from the sofa, snatched the little card from Reecie, and finished reading it. Evidently, there was something she didn't want me to hear. The look on her face said it all. As she perused the words on the card, I eased up on her and pulled the card out of her hand the way she did Reecie.

"Hey!" she reached out. I skipped over the words, jumping right to the sender.

"Adrian!" I hollered at her. She cringed in fear when I lunged forward. I wasn't going to hit her, but I did grab the roses and slam them forcefully to the floor, scattering petals everywhere.

"Why did you do that?" she cried out. Reecie didn't know what to make of our spat, so she ran out of the room after my violent outburst.

"You have some nerve asking me anything. What I should be asking you is what's going on? Why is somebody named Adrian sending flowers to our home?"

"He's a friend," was all she could come up with.

"Seems like more than a friend to me. Does he know you're married? Probably not. For anyone to be bold enough to send flowers here, he had to feel comfortable enough to do it."

"I don't know what made him do it."

"Oh, you know. Let me see your phone." It was on the coffee table.

"No, Carl!" I got my hands on it before she could reach for it. I scrolled through the numbers both received and sent, noticing a series of the same number. Wasn't quite sure what I was trying to pull off, but I was determined to discover something so I dialed the number and a male voice answered.

"I see you received my gift. How do you like them?" he asked in a seductive tone.

"Well, I believe my wife liked them very much, but I didn't care for them at all." Then I ended the call.

"Carl, give me my phone back." She went for it, but I smacked her hand away. I wasn't through with my investigation. I needed to see who this guy was and if I had to bet, I was sure there was a picture somewhere in that phone.

I flipped through the gallery, and it didn't take long for me to see what I was looking for. A light brown-skinned man with a muscular build posed in a few shots that were sent to her. I also saw a couple of pictures of my wife, obviously ones she had sent him. Looking closer at his face, there was something vaguely familiar about him. I'd seen him recently, but couldn't put my finger on it. Sandra could see my wheels turning, trying to figure it out. Then it hit me.

"Can I have my phone back now?" she asked humbly. I threw it at her feet, giving her a glare that could melt ice.

"Really, Sandra? An inmate at the prison?" I just walked past her without another look. At that point, I couldn't stand the sight of her.

"Carl, I can explain!" she called out.

"Don't bother." I needed a drink.

CHAPTER FOURTEEN

COOKIE

I didn't know whether to be mad at Adrian for sending the flowers unannounced, mad at Carl for going through my phone, or mad at myself for causing all of this to happen. My worst fear was confirmed when I saw the utter disappointment and hurt on Carl's face. Even though I'd experienced my share of hurt over the years from him making me feel like an incapable matter, treating me like an accessory to him at the church, the last thing I wanted was for Carl to call Adrian. I can't imagine how he felt hearing his voice instead of mine when he called. The sinister look on Carl's face showed that he loved every minute of busting me out. Deep down, I knew he was hurt; he just chose to hurt me first.

He didn't come home last night and there was no

telling what was going through his mind. Between the two of us, there were so many emotions on the table, and we hadn't dealt with any of our issues. We really should've gone to counseling when we had a chance. Now, I was afraid it was too late. The problems were mounting faster than we can find answers.

"What do you mean he has a son?" The shock hit my mom like it did me when Chloe broke the news.

"I was just as surprised as you. To hold something like that for all these years, it makes me wonder what else he could have hidden in the closet." I didn't want to mention the suspicious email I had stumbled across some weeks ago. Mom had been team Carl for as long as I could remember.

"Well, maybe there's a logical reason why he has kept this from you. Sometimes, it's not good to let your left hand know what your right is doing."

"Mom, you're not making sense. I'm his wife; something like this should be told to me. Secrets aren't meant to strengthen marriages, they weaken them. And whose side are you on anyway?"

"Cookie, you know I've always been fond of Carl. Marriages have problems. I would love for you to work through this one."

"This one is a bit much. It sounds like you're asking me to overlook the fact that Carl has had a son in hiding for our entire marriage."

"Well...I'm just saying."

"Thanks Mom, you've been a lot of help. I think I'll solve this one on my own."

"Whatever you do, try not to lose that husband of yours; getting anything better than a Pastor will be hard."

"You act like I'm at fault here. What if this was the other way around? His mother would be dragging me through the mud. You, on the other hand, are giving him a pass."

"Cookie, it's not that I'm giving him a pass, I just want you to look into all the circumstances. There has to be some reason; may not have had a choice. Carl doesn't seem like the type to keep secrets."

"Oh, you obviously don't know Carl like I do."

"Max, I actually was having a debate with my own mother about whether my husband is justified for secretly having a son."

"Your mom is a trip. I remember some of the things you were explaining to me at the beginning of our sessions."

"You don't know the half, girl."

"And you still haven't confronted Carl yet?"

"Ah, no. I'm in a bit of hot water with him right now."

"Wait a minute, I thought he was the one in hot water."

My session with Maxine was much needed. It gave us an opportunity to speak freely in the comforts of her office.

She had a lot to discuss, as did I. Her court date was approaching quickly and we had to go over contingency plans in the event things went left. The threat of danger was still out there. When you're dealing with an evil element, you can never feel comfortable thinking you've eliminated the problem entirely. For us, we're dealing with an evil uncommon to use.

Max didn't know that I had the $50,000 on standby, just in case. My hope is that the judge shows her some mercy, maybe gives her probation. If the worst happens and he does order her to do time, then we will have a nest egg for her to deal with her defense. Personally, I need for her to make it through this, not only for my sake or hers, but also for her son.

"Well Max, he is in hot water as far as I'm concerned, but I had something happen that leveled the playing field a bit."

"What was that?"

"You remember me mentioning Adrian?"

"The guy from the prison?"

"Yeah, well he sent some roses to my house."

"Wow, what a sweet gesture."

"It was until Carl saw them." Her mouth nearly fell on the floor.

"Girl, what did he do?"

"He slammed them on the floor, then snatched my phone out my hand and started scrolling through my numbers and pictures."

"Oh my God! You didn't have anything in there, did you?"

"His number was repetitive, so he tried it and got lucky."

"You mean he called Adrian? He had some nerve."

"I think at that point, he was reaching at straws. When he made contact and started talking, that's what made my heart sink."

"What could they have to talk about?"

"Carl said something slick, then the call ended."

"Cookie, you always have some drama going on," Max joked.

"Me? What about you? Court case pending. Gangsters trying to hunt you down, your life is scripted like a hip hop video." We both cracked up laughing at our tumultuous lives.

"You had to remind me just how screwed up my situation is."

"Max, don't even dwell on that. I have faith that the mountain that seems to be in front you will be crumbled to sand. Trust me, by the end of all this, you will come out smelling like a rose."

"How are you so sure?" I may not show it, but I'm scared to death."

"What does the bible teach about worrying?"

"Cookie, you know I'm not as far along in my faith as you are."

"In Matthew, it's speaking about how the lilies in the

field don't worry about how they will receive water, the birds in the air don't worry about how they will get fed. It says to deal with today, tomorrow has enough trouble of its own."

"Wow, that's in there?"

"There's an answer for every situation in the bible. You have to open up to the spirit and let it lead you."

"Not to change subjects, but what are you gonna do about Adrian?"

"I don't know yet. I haven't talked with him yet since the call. I'm not sure how he is feeling."

"You care about him, don't you?"

"I do, Max. I do."

Gabriel had been on my mind lately, but for different reason. I was really concerned about his progress. His recovery was important to me. He was a great athlete from the game or two that I saw, and the only reason he was hurting was because of me. I would feel horrible if he couldn't play up to the level he was at before. I called him to check on him, and he told me he was doing some physical therapy at his spot in Crofton.

"How is it going?"

"I'm coolin', just getting this therapy thing together. Once again, I appreciate you putting up the check for the whole process. They really treating me like a king up in here, all expenses paid for. I see you're a woman of her word."

"I try to be. And I told you, I got this taken care of because you went out there for me."

"For me, all in a day's work. As far as being shot, who knows, don't feel bad because of that."

"I do, though. If it wasn't for me, you wouldn't be in this position. What are the doctors saying?"

"Doc said the bullet went through my leg, causing minimal damage. There was a lot of blood loss and I had to have surgery to repair some muscle tissue that was ripped up." His casual description was gory.

"Ouch! That sounds bad."

"Not really. Hell, I was asleep through the whole process. This is the hard part right here, getting my leg back in the shape. I've been laying up, got to get back into basketball shape. I feel bad that I let me team down; we were having such a good season."

My heart went out to him. This young man had just been shot in a situation that could have gone drastically worse, and here he was, concerned about being a better teammate. That's what youth did for you.

"Well, I hope you're able to get back out there and do what you love. I'm sure Chloe would love to see you play again; she says she hasn't heard from you. What's up with that?"

"I kinda got my eyes on someone else," he gave me a flirtatious wink. No way this was happening. He was a kid, only a year older than my daughter. "C'mon, Ms. Andrews..."

"That's Mrs. Andrews," I stated emphatically.

"Okay, Mrs. Andrews. You can't deny the chemistry we have. When I was up in that hospital, thinking about how we came together to pull that off..."

"But Gabriel..."

"Then when you came to visit and prayed for me, I realized at that moment it was you I should be pursuing, not settling for Chloe," he continued to reflect.

"Hold on, Gabriel. Although I'm flattered, this is my daughter who is sitting at home, heartbroken because you are not returning her calls. That girl thinks the world of you and as much as I was against it at first, I think you have the potential to be a good young man for her."

"That's just it, I believe I'm ready to graduate to dating women older than me and the way we've connected, shoot...why not give it a chance?"

"Weren't you the same one that had your homeboys kidnap me? Men don't do that to women."

"I thought you forgave me for that? Besides, that was just a situation. I see different now, I see a future with us."

"I'm married, Gabriel, did you forget that part?" I had to remind him of the obvious.

"I know you are. Ain't nothing wrong with a young man on the side. Chloe told me you not really getting none in the bed, so maybe I can help Stella get her groove back." He smiled mischievously, and that signaled my exit. I couldn't believe he was bold enough to try to put moves on me, and I found it harder to believe that Chloe would put our personal business out like that. I turned to leave without saying another word. It was evident I had made a mistake by coming here. I picked up my pace as I headed for the door. He hollered at me.

"Just think about it!"

CHAPTER FIFTEEN

Adrian

I never expected the Pastor to call me from her phone. When I saw the number I just knew it was Cookie responding to my romantic gesture. Hearing his voice sent chills through me. This was the same man I looked eye to eye just a few nights ago. I was so tempted to call back hoping she would answer, but I opted against it, fearing it would make things bad for her.

Going into detail that morning felt strange. I had plenty of things to keep me occupied, but my mind was focused on Cookie. When I walked into counseling the whole atmosphere seemed off. Was it me or was everyone moving in fast forward. Counselors were busying around, there was a room full of new arrivals waiting to be seen and Pam was taking calls like she was a telemarketer.

She saw me walk by and summoned me with a finger

while still holding the phone to her ear. Before I went to start my duties I stepped into her office. Pam ended her call and diverted her attention to me.

"Adrian, what's been going on with you lately? The past week or so you've come in here with a funk not to mention you haven't called me none this weekend."

I really didn't pay much attention to my actions, but with her pointing it out made me realize how much she's been missing me. It probably hard to see me through the week and control her emotions with hopes of releasing them over the phone with me. My time has gone to the pursuit of Cookie.

It's crazy when you crave the forbidden fruit when the healthy fruit is right there before you. Human nature tells you to go after what you can't have. Pam was an example of a farm fresh vegetable, good for consumption, but I had the fattened, calorie filled piece of steak in my sights and couldn't wait to sink my teeth in it.

"You listening to me?" She snapped me out of my wandering thoughts. My mind was still on what my next move was with Cookie. The roses were supposed to be checkmate; instead, I feel like I made a bad move that got me trapped up.

"Yea. I apologize for not getting with you, my mind has been on a lot of different things."

"Obviously."

"I'll tighten up, Pam, okay?" She gave me those eyes, the ones that initially drew me in.

"You better," she teased, completely forgetting that she was in her place of business, a room full of nosey inmates not even fifteen feet away.

"I know you probably need some more cigs, I had to chill for a minute after the library incident," she explained.

I didn't ask her for that, but I guess she felt somewhat guilty thinking that was the reason I had pulled back from our emotional encounters. "I totally understand. You got to be safe. Whenever is good with me."

That interaction was enough to satisfy her for the moment. I stepped out as she took another call. As soon as I opened the utility closet, the outside door stormed open with four Drop Squad members rushing in. The Drop Squad was a security crew the Warden assembled to patrol the compound, conducting shakedowns, locking down inmates—pretty much maintain order. They walk around wearing all black with pellet guns holstered on their hips. They usually arrive when situations get serious so I wondered who they were here to take down.

"Upshaw!" the first one barked. "Step out and put your hands on the wall!" At this point all eyes were on one. Counselors came out to see what the commotion was about, the inmates turned to see the show, even Pam peeked out in horror when she saw me being appre-hended. I was so embarrassed.

"What's up? What did I do?"

"Shut up and come with us!" another shouted, posi-tioning my arms so he could slam the handcuffs on me.

They walked me out, and all I could think about on the way was what kind of answers I could give. It would help if I knew what my infraction was, but I had to be prepared for the worst. Maybe someone snitched on me about my phone. Or somebody caught wind of the dealings Pam and I had; people were always watching. This might not even have anything to do with me; they could be trying to scare me into snitching on someone else for something, but what?

Instead of going to the hole, we went to the security office, where the sergeant of the squad awaited me.

"Take the cuffs off of him," he ordered. "He's done nothing wrong, at least not what we can prove." Now, I was totally confused. What was he talking about? What kind of mind games was he playing?

"Look, Upshaw, do you know why we picked you up?" I had to be careful how I answered. It could be a trick.

"No, not a clue."

"Are you sure?" What is this, an inquisition?

"Yes, I'm sure."

"Well, we got a call from Pastor Andrews, do you know who that is?" I gave him silence as my answer, so he continued.

"He says an inmate at this facility sent his wife, First Lady Sandra Andrews, some roses." I smiled at the allegation.

"Do you think this is funny, son? This is very serious."

"I'm sorry sir, but do you realize that in order to send

flowers to someone, you have to know the address to the person, not to mention locating a florist," I finally spoke.

"You think that's impossible? Upshaw, I'm not new to this, you inmates can do amazing things with the use of a cell phone."

"Very true. And best believe, if I did have access to a phone, delivering flowers would not be on my agenda. Finding a way out of this prison would be priority." My rebuttal gave him reason to ponder.

"I hope, for your sake, you stand by your story because I have a crew of my boys down in your dorm tearing your shit up. And if I find a shred of evidence that leads me to believe that you and this man's wife are interacting, then I will make you disappear for a long time."

His threat was loud, but fell on deaf ears. I had nothing in my possession that would link me to Cookie. Oh, and the phone? They would never find. When I got back to the dorm, sure enough, my area looked like a disaster zone. Preacherman was the first one to greet me at my bunk; he couldn't even sit in his favorite spot because there was so much of my stuff scattered all over the bed.

"Bro, they went through everything. We couldn't get nowhere near your bed."

"I know, Preach. Sarge told me that his crew was here. He had me in cuffs in his office."

"For real? What was he talking about?"

"Man, he was interrogating me, trying to get me to break. I'm just glad I keep things straight here."

"Well, they confiscated some of your legal work and that folder you keep on your middle shelf, they must went to go through your mail."

"Probably. I'm not worried, though. Let them do what they gotta do; eventually, they will give my stuff back."

"What made them come down on you in the first place?"

"Long story, my friend, long story."

Pastor Andrews really went to the extreme to get me jammed up. Him calling down here forced this administration to respond, and they did expediently. I will probably be under investigation for a couple of weeks, which I'm not worried about. However, it will be awkward when the church group returns next month. I'm quite sure the Pastor will make a return appearance.

After about a week, I could tell the situation had died down a bit by the way everyone was moving. I continued going to detail as usual, but really didn't speak to anyone about the incident. Of course, Pam was overly concerned, wondering why they came in there like that. I was evasive, giving her vague answers. Telling the truth would send her into an emotional whirlwind, leading to more questions I wasn't prepared to answer.

With all the commotion I caused in counseling, it was a wonder how I even had my detail. There are people lined up to get in my position and I'm sure there was somebody waiting in the wings saying something foul about me.

"So are you gonna tell me what happened or are you

gonna keep beating around the bush?" Pam popped up on me in the utility closet when I was cleaning out a mop. I had my back to her so I couldn't see the distraught expression on her face.

"I already told you why they came, Sergeant wanted some information on a situation and I wouldn't cooperate."

"And it took all of that?" Why was your name involved?"

"Pam, there's nothing to worry about." I looked her in the eyes trying to reassure her. She let up, but I have a feeling she wasn't through with her questioning.

"Is that why you haven't contacted me?"

"That's exactly why. I had to wait for the dust to settle around here. It just wasn't safe to have the phone out."

"I definitely understand that. Adrian?" Her soft tone weakened me.

"Yes."

"Can you hold me?" I took her in my arms, held her tight giving her a comfort she'd been longing for. Before she left she leaned in and kissed me, her eyes twinkled with hope, my heart was filled with uncertainty.

CHAPTER SIXTEEN

Carl

The sun peeking through the cumulus clouds seemed to shine a little brighter over the church today. When I pulled into my parking space, it felt good to see my parking sign standing tall reminding me of all the hard work I've put in. My staff has been a huge support and a large reason for my success, but my wife and first lady is the one responsible for me achieving my goals.

At the beginning, she was behind me on every decision, beside me when the opposition was against me, and ahead of me on innovative ideas that proved to benefit the church. Our partnership had been instrumental in our growth, so it was troubling to know that our partnership at home was in danger. Sometimes, I felt the only thing keeping us together was the children. If it weren't for them, we'd probably be done.

So for us to be on such a different path was disturbing. I had big plans for us; next up for me, becoming a Bishop, then I'd pursue political office. Problem is, I hadn't had the chance to sit down and explain her role in these plans. Every time I approached the subject, she always went in another direction. The support she showed at the start of our relationship had dissipated.

Walking into my office, I noticed a stack of paperwork on my desk that needed to be looked over. As I fingered through the first few pages, my secretary came through the door seemingly upset.

"Pastor, this man was up here early this morning demanding to see you. He made such a disturbance, I thought I'd have to call the police, but he agreed to calm down and come back later. Well, later is now."

"Who is this man?"

"He says he is your son."

Oh boy, here we go again. He definitely had to stop with these public scenes. I was going to have to face him and find out exactly what was on his mind. If I didn't get a handle on this, the outcome could come back to bite me square in the behind.

"Where is he now?"

"I told him he was welcome to wait in the chapel area, he said that would be fine."

I made my way from my office, through the vestibule, entering the room where every Sunday morning, God used me to deliver His message. So why did I feel awkward in my own comfort zone? Seeing the back of his head made me instantly feel like a stranger relinquishing the power to him.

"I know you would eventually show up," he said without even turning to see me.

I wondered how he knew it was me who entered. There was no one else in there as he sat alone in one of the pews. "I can tell by the way you walk. I have the same walk, it's in your genes."

Taking a seat next to him, I turned to face him before I spoke. "What is it you want from me?"

"You don't sound very welcoming."

"That's because I'm still trying to figure out what your intentions are."

"I don't want anything from you, if that's what you're thinking. No money. What I want is something you can give freely."

"And what's that?"

"Love. I just want a relationship with you, Dad."

Hearing him calling me "Dad" still had an uneasy sound to it. Not that what he was asking is out of the question; it just came out of nowhere, he came out of nowhere."

"Carl, I have a family and we...well, we haven't been in contact with each other in a long time."

"Try never. That's why I think it would be a good idea to start with a cordial relationship. Maybe I could come through and meet the rest of your family."

"I don't think that would be a good idea."

"Why not?"

"Yeah, why not, Carl?" The voice seemed to echo off the walls in the sanctuary; it was a familiar voice, at that.

"Sandra...uh, what are you doing here?" As the words left my lips, I completely forgot about the staff meeting I had scheduled for today.

"If I'm not mistaken, I have every right to be here, don't you think?" She approached with the subtlety of a bull in a store made of crystal. When she came into our space, the awkwardness was felt between the three of us.

"Of course you do, it's just I wasn't expecting you this early."

"I can see what. You probably would've rescheduled this little meeting." Before I could utter a response, she interrupted me.

"Hi, I'm Sandra Andrews, Carl's wife."

"Oh, I know who you are, it's nice to meet you."

"Now, that's interesting. How is it that you know who I am, but I've never heard of you? Carl, can you answer that?" We both went to speak simultaneously, then I started to explain when she gave us an incredulous look.

"Both our names are Carl. Sandra, this is Carl Andrews, Jr."

The silence was as haunting as Freddy Krueger in his prime. "He is my son."

"Carl, my husband, I'm so glad you chose to enlighten

me. It's a shame that I had to find out this information from someone other than you."

"What? Who told you?" Carl Jr . looked as if to say *not me.*

"Who told is not important. The question is, why was this hidden from me for so long? Our whole marriage together, and you've had a son. And it's apparent that this happened before me."

"Sandra, there's a lot to explain."

"Mrs. Andrews, to his defense, for some years, I lost contact with him. Didn't reach out to him 'til recently."

"Don't try to cover for him. His irresponsibility is not to be covered up by excuses. Carl knows he has had plenty of opportunities to let me know about you, isn't that right, Carl?"

Now, she was patronizing me in front of my son, as if I was her son. I was still a grown man, head of my household, and leader of this church. I'm not sure what she was trying to prove by trying to chastise me in front of Carl, but it was downright demeaning to be publicly berated.

"Sandra, this is hardly the place to discuss your grievance."

"I think this is precisely the place; at least here, dishonesty will cause a ton of guilt."

"Can we just discuss this at home?"

"Sure, let's do that."

"Hey, what about me? When do I get to lodge my issues? Dad, how can we establish a relationship?"

"I really don't know. Right now, my head is going in a million different directions."

"Well, I'll be right here when you figure out which way you plan to go." It may sound cruel, but why did he pick now to come and disrupt my life? I had enough issues going on as it was; this just complicated matters worse.

Throughout our staff meeting, I could feel Sandra's eyes searing through me. It was obvious that what had transpired earlier had really upset her. We had a lot of ground to cover, so I kept my composure. My gut was secretly hoping she wouldn't air my dirty laundry in front of everybody. At this point, I couldn't put anything past her.

"Brother Powers, I hear the officials over at Lofton State Prison are really impressed with the level of professionalism you're displaying when you go in for service. Not only is your message strong, but you are representing Victory in Faith to the highest extent."

"Thank you, Pastor," he said, beaming with pride.

"I also want to acknowledge our music director for his dedication to making sure the choir is in order. Music is important to our services, it ushers in the spirit. The way you assembled the band to create the sound you do is something to marvel at. Thumbs up for finding that keyboard player, too."

"Thank you very much, Pastor." He smiled at the accolades he just received.

I looked over and noticed my wife and Sister Allen

whispering amongst themselves, then she pulled her cell phone out and pointed something out to Sandra. Her eyes opened wide, then peered at me with a look so sinister, you'd think I said something disrespectful about her mother. Whatever it was, I was sure I would hear about it later.

I retreated back to my office after the meeting, more so to collect my thoughts. This day started off rocky, heading south and it wasn't even 2 o'clock yet. I looked at my computer screen and noticed an email unopened. Clicking on the envelope, I started to read its contents After the first line, I felt an uneasiness in my stomach. I wondered when the madness would end, but had to realize it was a madness that I caused. The words staring back at me were haunting.

Carlton, this feeling I have for you is turning me crazy. I really don't know how we got to this point, but something needs to be done. In every other part of my life, I'm in control; however, with you, I feel powerless. I know all the things that make you strong and the things that weaken you. I'm at a stage now where I really don't care about the consequences, and it's obvious you don't care about my feelings. Problem is, you got me here. You have impacted my life, at first it was a positive way, but now it's turned negative. I can't function and it's not fair that you've just moved on with your life, leaving me in this state of confusion. Come meet me so we can discuss how we're going to handle this. If you don't show, then there will be signs of my fury. I hate to do this, please don't force me to.

There was an address and a meeting time. I didn't like ultimatums or idle threats, yet this seemed real. This could turn out to be detrimental to not only my family, but to my reputation as a Pastor.

CHAPTER SEVENTEEN

COOKIE

All I saw coming down the hallway was streak then Carl flying out of his office. He was so focused on what was on his mind he didn't even notice me or the fact that he left his door open. It wasn't like me to invade people's privacy, but lately I haven't been much like myself. So I decided to peek in his office and take a look around. After what I was on Sister Allen's phone my suspicion was running high and everything was fair game.

True enough I was running the risk of getting caught, that's the chance you take when things in your life are in dismay. For me it was worth it. Besides, if Carl didn't have anything to hide there wouldn't be anything to worry about. The way he'd been acting I believe there are plenty of skeletons in his closet.

Shuffling through some papers on his desk, there was

nothing but invoices, memorandums, and other church related items. Nothing of any significant interest surfaced so I moved my search to his laptop. The login screen was still showing, arrow pointing toward the password. I hoped he hadn't changed it. I typed in *John 3:16*.

Just as I pressed enter, I heard a familiar tune coming from my pocket. I chose "Optimistic" by the Sounds of Blackness as my ringtone to be a constant inspiration, but at that moment, it scared the life out of me. When I looked at the screen, I saw it was Max.

"Damn girl, you scared the hell out of me!"

"What are you doing?"

"I'm in Carl's office investigating. He's away from the church, so I'm crunched for time."

"You're at the church cursing like that?" She chuckled.

"The way I'm feeling, somebody has hell to pay. I'm just making a down payment." She laughed harder.

"You said investigating? What are you looking for?"

"I think I just found it. Max, let me call you back."

I ended the call and began to read the opened email. The words were hard to digest, but pretty much confirmed what I saw on Sister Allen's phone earlier. Social media could be the destroyer of lives, depending on how viral the subject matter went. The way this may play out, our sacred bond may be in jeopardy. That's only if there was any truth to this.

I closed the laptop and tried to arrange everything

back the way it was. Exiting the office, I ran dead into Deacon Pryor.

"Oh, I'm sorry Deacon. I didn't see you."

His hard muscular build halted my progress like a cement wall. I pushed back off of him just enough to see the lustful gaze in his eyes. I heard rumors around the church that he had a crush on me, and I tried my best to not be put in situations with him. Well, this was definitely awkward.

"Well, I've been seeing," he said flirtatiously.

"Deacon Pryor, honestly I'm flattered, but I don't think the Pastor would approve of your advances."

"I won't tell if you won't tell." He winked.

"Have a good day, Deacon," I said, brushing past him. I didn't have time to entertain him. On an ordinary day, I probably would've made it absolutely clear that what he was doing was inappropriate not only in the eyes of my husband, but also in the eyes of God.

It seems like I missed my calling; with all this following around and investigative work, I should've been a detective. After seeing the address on the email, I was on a mission to make a bust. Something very suspicious was going on with Carl and this mysterious meeting, but I was going to get to the bottom of it today.

"I'm glad you called back, Cookie, I'm beginning to worry about you."

"Worry? Why you say that?"

"You have a lot of things causing you stress in your life right now. As your therapist and friend, I'm concerned."

"I'll be alright, Max. I feel like I'm living a lie. There are a lot of hidden truths going on in this marriage."

"On both sides," she stated flatly, and the weight of those words sank deep. "There are things you're keeping from Carl, too. The reality is, if neither of you are willing to fix what's wrong, then you guys are headed for destruction."

"We're headed in different directions, for sure. Me talking to Adrian is evidence of that. Max, my body is in that house, but it seems like everything else, my spirit, my commitment, my heart—all that is drifting away. These secrets that keep popping up aren't helping matters any."

"What secrets?"

"That's what I'm going to find out now. Carl is due to meet with some mystery woman, according to the email I read on his laptop."

"See, you're sneaking around his office, snooping on his laptop."

"If he didn't give me just cause, then I wouldn't have to do it."

"Understandable. Just remember, every action has a consequence."

"I realize that. I'm searching for the answers that will give me clarity on which way I need to go."

"Be careful, you may find something you didn't want to see."

My phone conversation with Maxine carried me all the way to my destination. The address led me downtown to a restaurant in Dupont Circle. I wondered why this location was chosen. There was nothing but shopping boutiques and clubs, mostly catering to the gay community. The evidence was all the nightlife advertisements adorning the light poles and empty wall spaces.

I parallel parked across the street, right in front of *Club Hydro*. Ever since marijuana had been legalized in the District, spots like this had popped up all over town, allowing people to congregate and smoke. Now, it was legal to walk around in a high-induced funk. It was amazing how much the world had changed over the years. The way we smoked weed in the late '70s, we would've loved to live in these times.

Frankie's was quaint, almost unnoticeable from the street front. When I walked in, the atmosphere was dark and gloomy, far from what I would consider an upbeat meeting place. In fact, if you were trying to be secretive, this was the place to be. There were a lot of booths lining the back wall along with a couple of privacy areas, probably reserved for VIP.

I had the receptionist seat me in a secluded section, somewhere I could see the whole room. My mind was hardly on eating, but I did order an appetizer to not appear obvious that I was there spying. Keeping my eyes peeled, I saw no signs of Carl or his rendezvous companion. At first,

I thought maybe I had read the address wrong, then I saw him.

Sauntering across the room coming from the direction of the restroom came Carlton Andrews, the powerful man of the cloth, the father of my children, and the man I had pledged to spend the rest of my life with. The question that had been lingering in my mind was, who was the bitch he was stepping out on me with?

Max did have a point; who was I to be angry with Carl when I, too, had allowed my heart to drift? To me, my reasons were justified, so this was his chance to voice his reasons. After the confrontation this morning with this guy who claimed to be his son, then the activity on social media, now this clandestine meeting, my ears were wide open to any explanation he could offer up.

He eased over to a table in the back of the room. Before he sat down, he looked around to see if someone was watching him, yet another suspicious move. Then I witnessed something that appalled me. There was a man sitting opposite my husband, talking with animated gestures as if he was pleading with him about something. Carl appeared to be in defense mode to the gentleman's tirade. To the outside eyes, it could've been mistaken as a lover's quarrel.

I didn't want to let my mind go there, but the more I observed their discourse and interaction, the more there seemed to be something deeper going on. Carl attempted to comfort his emotions, which was working for the most part, but when his quest began to get irate, a full-blown argument ensued. So much attention was being drawn to them that the restaurant manager had to come and calm the situation down, threatening to throw them out. By this time, all attention was on them. I believe this was what he wanted because he stood, looked around, then raised his voice a level. "You should've never tried to get with me, Carl, if you planned to lead me on! Now, I'm going to make it my business to tell everyone you're a fraud." He turned on his heels and moved swiftly through the arrangement of tables leading toward the door.

"Patrick, wait!" Carl called out, now thoroughly embarrassed. This public display was the worst form of publicity, definitely damaging to anyone who was revered as a figure representing the church. With his aspirations of becoming a Bishop hanging in the balance, this was the last thing he needed. I, for one, was very shocked at the discovery that my husband of seventeen years was having an affair with a man.

Now, I understood there were two sides to every story, and I planned to hear his side out just as a formality, but a man didn't act out like that in the eyes of others, with so much emotion, if there wasn't some truth. This explained the email I read a few months ago and all the late nights at the church, and the feminine ways shown in the home. Hell, I was the only one that had been the fool.

CHAPTER EIGHTEEN

Adrian

"Where is everyone at?" I asked Pam as she called me into her office and drew the blinds closed. I had gotten called out to the library to handle some legal paperwork and returned to counseling. I had to lay some wax, which takes hours to dry as I knew that I would be there late this evening. When I entered, I noticed all the offices were locked, lights off, looking like everyone had left for the day.

"The whole staff took a half a day. It's the Thursday before a holiday weekend and everybody was talking about going to the Hampton/Howard homecoming game."

"Why aren't you going? That sounds like a blast. I wish I could get to that."

"Somebody had to stay back and do some work." She winked, then approached me.

"So, it's just you and me, huh?" I asked, focusing on the seductive look in her eyes.

"Yup, just you and me."

"Doing some work?" I took a step closer to her until I was invading her space.

"Tell me what you want to work on," she whispered and at that point, no more words were spoken.

I leaned in and kissed her passionately. Our tongues danced inside each other's mouths for what seemed like eternity until we came up for air. My hands probed over her back, then eased down to her ample back side. She looked at me seductively in the eye, then went to say something. Before she spoke, I read her body language, lifted her up off her feet, and placed her on the edge of her desk.

"Adrian, take me," she managed out breathlessly.

Without hesitation, I reached under her fitted skirt and slid her panties down and off. She opened her legs wider as an invitation into her paradise. And what a lovely one it was, neatly trimmed with barely a trace of pubic hair. Nearly on my knees, I buried my face in between her thighs, tasting her wetness. Her throbbing clitoris pulsated with each touch of my tongue against her willing flesh. The heat emanating from her was enough to show me she wanted more.

She sighed out her satisfaction, moaned her appreciation in the air. The more I pleased her, the more she pulled me in. There was no greater expression of pleasure than to hear her loud pants and soft tones echoing off her walls. Her plaques, certifications, and paintings were all in attendance to witness the show I was performing. When she sang out in ecstasy, I knew I had a sensitive spot. Her eruption was clear evidence that she had made it to the peak and was rolling downhill.

"Oh, Adrian," she moaned. While Pam was still in a state of bliss, I wanted to join her on that level. Pulling her skirt all the way up, I was able to fully spread her legs and enter her. At first, my nerves were boiling over. We were going at it like we were in the comfort of the Embassy Suites, having a sexual escapade. Yet in reality, we were in the forbidden zone, Pam's secluded office. At any moment, this great experience could turn tragic if someone were to discover us.

For Pam, it seemed like the threat of being caught excited her. I felt the increase in passion through her touch. Her fingers clenched into my shirt, trying desperately to reach my skin. My third eye's awareness was still alert to an unexpected interruption; someone had to drive this car that was coming dangerously close to careening off the road. Pam was obviously too intoxicated in her own lust to handle the wheel.

Our flesh met the deeper I went and the closer we got, the more we wanted each other to erupt. I'm sure she was content with extending our love making, but I was more concerned with our safety rather than fulfilling our sexual desires. As I increased my thrusts, Pam's moans became contagious; she urged me to be more audible. My concentration was on completing the task at hand, then getting out of harm's way.

I felt Pam release her climax with a loud exhale. Her eyes were closed, totally oblivious to where we were. For all she knew, we were held up in the comfort of her bedroom, waiting for the early morning sun to shine through the blinds. I knew better. Even though I reached my peak as well, it didn't take long for me to regain my faculties. It was a good thing, too.

"Pam, put your panties on and pull your shirt down, hurry up!" I ordered while straightening myself up. I'd learned to always keep one ear open in this environment, especially when I was in a situation where I could get jammed.

"Adrian, what's wrong?" she asked while doing as she was told.

"Shhh!" I quieted her, easing over to the door, now hearing what I suspected were voices in the office next to hers. My heart was racing like the Dayton 500, last lap, but I had to keep my composure. I had to think. How long had they been here? Did they see or hear anything suspicious when they came in? Pam was pretty loud when she climaxed.

"What is it?" she asked again, coming over to me. I went into action.

"Okay look, slowly open the blinds to your office, then take some files into the hallway and walk by the other office. Act as if you didn't know they were there, I mean show complete shock on your face.

"Okay," was all she said, then did as I told her. I stood near the door, heart still pounding, listening for the response.

"Oh my God! You guys scared me. I thought everyone was gone for the weekend," Pam shrieked out, putting on her best acting job; it was working.

"Oh hey Pam, girl Ron was just accompanying me back here so I can send these emails to the central office. I was supposed to do it this morning, but got distracted somehow; ain't that right, Ron?" I heard the voice of the other woman. It was Counselor Simpson, the plus sized woman who always wore tight, revealing clothing, the kind that showed all her curves and several other features she probably didn't plan on showing. For inmates who weren't accustomed to seeing women, it would be very enticing but to the staff, it came off as inappropriate attire. This Ron guy must be her man, which I had no clue she even had. In all actuality, she was in violation for having him inside the gates. She was violating the ethical and safety codes of the prison, but because Officer Clark at the front gate was her best friend, she tended to get away with things others didn't.

"So. this is the mystery man we've been hearing about?" Pam kept the conversation directed at Ms. Simpson, knowing she loved talking about herself and this man of hers.

"Yes, girl," she exclaimed.

"Just be careful, you know how these folks are around here, they'll tell on their own mommas and not think twice about it."

"Pam, I got it covered. What you doing here this late anyway?" I heard her ask. I hoped Pam had a clear answer to ward off suspicion.

"You know today's my late day, I got stuck doing the files."

"I hate the late days; it keeps me from doing what I want to do, like being with my boo."

"I know that's right. Well, let me get these things copied. Y'all be careful getting out of here, you never know who's watching."

"I'll be on the lookout."

Pam came back in her office and signed relief. Not too long after, we heard the outside door close and lock.

"Whoo, that was close."

"Too close, it could be really bad if we get caught doing anything." She came up on me and stroked the side of my face.

"Aww Adrian, you're a smart man," she said teasingly. I removed her hand, then gave her a serious look.

"We both have to be smart about what we do. The consequences are great for the both of us."

"I have the utmost trust in you, Adrian, and when you get out, I know you will take care of me, the same way you do in here." Her words pierced me. Was she getting serious? I didn't know how to take what she just said, so I let her words hang in the air with no response. I gathered my things, leaving her office. I left out of the building without even doing the floor. Something in her eyes triggered me to distance myself. I'm sure she was caught up in the moment and allowed her emotions to take control, but I was more concerned with our well-being, not letting the moment override our judgment. Different lanes produced different results. Until I was sure about her intentions, I had to fall back from Pam and her advances. The paperwork I received and signed off on in the library was enough to get me to refocus. I didn't even get a chance to share the news with her.

"A.U, we've been wondering where you've been." Preach met me at my bunk when I made it in. It had been a long day and all I wanted was a shower. My night would be complete when I got a chance to speak with Cookie.

"I had to stay late to do the floor in counseling." I couldn't tell Preach I never got to do the floor because that would draw another set of questions I wasn't prepared to answer.

"What's going on up in here?"

"Man, you know there's always something going on. Your boy, Richie Rich, came back from court."

"Yeah, he was hoping to get his case overturned."

"Yup, there was a witness on his case who was due to testify on his behalf; that evidence alone would've gotten his whole joint thrown out. But the judge realized she was lying on the stand."

"How did he know that?"

"She had originally given a statement attesting to the crime she witnessed, so when they had this retrial, evidently she changed her story up. The judge showed her the original statement, then cited her for perjury."

"What made her switch her testimony?"

"A little money influence will make you change a whole lot of things. Rich still has his crew out there, they're some straight up street dudes, so the money is definitely available. She may have been in a bad spot and needed some help. You never know what moves people. All I know is she made a choice to take the money and change her story, and it ended up landing her in jail. Rich said that woman cost him his chance at freedom and she has to pay. From the way he was looking, I don't think he was talking about the money she got from them."

After hearing Preach recount the situation with Richie Rich, I pieced it together, realizing the woman was the one Cookie had helped get out of jail. She was her friend and I hoped she knew how much trouble she could really be in. Rich's crew didn't play games. They were serious about their money and loyalty. I believe that in their eyes, this woman was disloyal, even though she tried to do as they asked. The fact that she didn't serve her purpose could her place in a lose-lose situation. My worry was that Cookie would end up tied into her mess.

CHAPTER NINETEEN

Carl

My life had been turned completely upside down. After being thoroughly embarrassed in public at that Dupont Circle restaurant, I had a long road ahead to recover from the incident. Sandra hasn't spoken to me since that day; in fact, we weren't even sleeping in the same room. The tension in the house was as thick as a porterhouse steak. My family at home had been affected by my choices. I just hoped the church family was a bit more forgiving.

"Reecie, you want to ride with me over to the church?"

"Sure, Daddy." At first, she looked irritated at the interruption. She was watching one of her favorite television shows and normally, I didn't like disturbing her groove. I had to admit, I was looking for some alone time with my daughter. I know that was kind of selfish but the way the tide was shifting in my life, I sure didn't want to lose my baby girl in the midst of the storm. Besides, I tried Chloe earlier and she definitely didn't want to be bothered with me.

On the way over, there was an uncomfortable silence. Usually, we didn't have a problem with conversation. However, there was good reason for the dead space.

"So, how's school going?" I asked, trying to break the ice.

"You really want me to answer that question?" The scowl on her face was one that I had never seen before from her. My baby gave me a look of disgust which held something much deeper.

"Ah, yes, I'd like to know."

"Well, for starters, I've been totally humiliated by the things you've done."

"What things?" I tried to go the innocent route. It was apparent she was not happy with me playing on her intelligence.

"Do you even look at social media? It's posted all over the place that not only do you have a son, but you are having an affair on Mom."

Hearing those words coming from my little girl's mouth crushed me from the inside out. I wondered how long this had been floating on the social networks. Even worse, how many people had viewed it? It was obvious that Sandra knew; she and Sister Allen were probably viewing it during our staff meeting. Her showing up at the restaurant was just to gain confirmation.

"I'm not going to even lie, Reecie, I don't pay too much attention to the rumors on the internet."

"Well, that's the problem because the rest of the world does. It's already hard being a pastor's daughter, but now with this. I'm catching hell from all angles." She caught herself cursing, covering her mouth.

"Alright, young lady, watch your language. I'm still your father and I deserve that much respect."

"Respect went out the window when you did what you did, ad." I really didn't have anything to say. She had every right to feel resentment toward me. Reecie was just a teenager and deserved the best chance to succeed. There was a tremendous amount of pressure on her having my last name. The more notoriety her mother and I attained, the harder it would be for Chloe and her.

When we arrived at the church, Reecie exited without saying a word. I didn't bother to catch up with her, just let her have her space. The vibe inside felt awkward; folks that usually cordially spoke were quiet. Instead, I got stares and looks of disgust from those who reward me.

Standing by my office was the Public Relations representative for the church, Mrs. Crowell. She only showed up if something was wrong.

"Let me guess, something's wrong," I stated flatly.

"Inside your office," she directed with a finger point, as if I was in trouble with the school principal. I took a seat behind my desk although the way things were looking, maybe I should have relinquished my seat to her.

"Pastor Andrews, I don't know if you realize it or not, but this situation you've gotten yourself into is very serious. Not only are you in jeopardy of losing credibility with your congregation, may I add, but you're also threatening any kind of future you have left in the ministry." Her words were haunting.

"What is it that I need to do?"

"Pastor, the damage has already been done."

"What's being said? I don't go on those social sites, too much gossip."

"Well, as it stands, you are the brunt of the gossip. Look so you can see for yourself." She pulled out her phone; by the size of it, I thought she was carrying around a flat screen television. She scrolled and swiped the screen until she got to what she wanted me to see.

"Here, check this out." There was an instant message posted to anyone who would read it:

I hope you know your pastor as well as you think you do. His job is to lead you to greener pastures, make sure he doesn't lead you over a cliff instead. Hypocrisy is almost as bad as false prophecy; in my eyes, he is both. He will lead you on the same way he did me. There's no Victory in his faith, you will be a loser if you believe in him.

"That could be directed to anyone. Those were just hurtful words from a damaged soul." She gave me a look of unbelief.

"How can you be so naïve?" Ok, well there's more." She scrolled down until she came to a video. She pressed play, and there was Patrick's face. He must've made the video after he threatened me on the phone that day I had stood him up. He was adamant about meeting with me, but that was the day Carl, Jr. unexpectedly popped up. I completely forgot, but evidently he didn't.

This image must've been what made people take notice; he appeared to be hurt and desperate. Listening to his tone, I could hear the surety in his words. He was confessing his adoration for me and making it seem like we had a serious relationship going on. The way he conveyed his message, no one who came across it wouldn't think otherwise, and I believe that was his intent.

"Now, do you see how this makes you look? Whoever this man is, he is infatuated with you and if he can't have you, he is out to ruin you. It looks like he's doing a pretty good job to me."

"I'm speechless. I have to address this somehow, at least clear things with the church."

"I don't think that will be a good idea."

"What do you mean? The people need to know the truth."

"Right now, this is their truth. How do you plan on convincing the public that you aren't cheating on the First Lady with a man?"

"But I'm not! This is not the truth!" I shouted.

"I'm sorry, Pastor. In this day and age, people are so

driven by gossip and drama that they'd rather believe what they perceive as the truth than the actual truth itself."

"That's just crazy." I was so frustrated with her analysis, I left like I was in therapy.

"This whole situation is crazy. And we haven't even covered how you're gonna handle this son that has everyone around here talking."

"He has been showing up lately, either here or at my home," I explained.

"What is it that he wants? I mean, besides making your world uncomfortable."

"I'm not quite sure. He says all he wants is a relationship with me and my family. I don't see how that's going to be possible because my family is in full dysfunction. My oldest daughter has gone silent on me, my youngest seems so disappointed in me that she's headed that way also."

"Yeah, I saw her earlier. She doesn't look like she's taking it well. It's understandable. She's young and has this impression of you that's pure and innocent. It's stained like blood on a white dress."

"My wife is probably experiencing the worst of it. She walked in on my son and I having a heated discussion in the sanctuary. Her reaction was odd, as if she was already informed of the news. Whatever the case, her whole mood changed from that day forth."

"That kind of news would be traumatic to a wife whose husband vowed to never keep secrets."

"Well, I definitely didn't intend for her to see me and Patrick talking at a restaurant downtown."

"Hold on, wait a minute. What restaurant? And who is Patrick?"

I figured it was time to come clean about everything.

"Patrick is the guy on the video. He threatened to go public with the news that we were involved in a relationship if I didn't meet with him. I had been trying to avoid him, but I knew he would make good on the threat and I had way too much to lose not to see it through."

"And Sandra saw you guys talking? How did she know that you had a meeting?"

"I don't know. Patrick contacted me by email with the address. She must've logged in using our joint password. Damn, she's been snooping around in my office."

"Do you blame her?"

"I guess not."

Sandra had every right to be suspicious. The one person I wanted to get things straight with was her. It would be a long road to building trust and I wasn't sure if it would ever be restored but I'd have to start somewhere. Mrs. Crowell offered some good advice. We hired her to put out fires that would harm the church or its principal members, so she said she'd do her best to keep the press away from the grounds. She also suggested I write formal letters to the other Pastors and Bishops in the area explaining my wrongdoing. That way, they would hear it from the source instead of the twisted media.

One piece of advice I didn't follow was not addressing my congregation. I thought they should know that their Pastor had flaws. I was a human being striving for perfection; sometimes, we made mistakes along the way. The message I had for them was when you got knocked down, you got up. Let he who cast the first stone show himself sinless.

CHAPTER TWENTY

COOKIE

The same song kept playing over and over in my head. "Circles" by Atlantic Star played on the radio, etching the tune inside of me. My emotions were traveling in circles, a tornado touching down where it pleased. The stirring anger that was building for Carl was rivaled by the longing to be with Adrian.

My heart went out to him when I witnessed a sergeant getting on his case for neglecting to have the multipurpose room's floor buffed to a shine. It didn't really dawn on me how much time was put into the floor maintenance at the prison until I saw that it did lack its usual luster. Before our Friday service, Adrian explained his position to no avail. The superior officer continued to chastise him in front of us. To see that made me totally sympathetic to what Adrian had to endure daily.

The service went well and when I looked in the crowd, I could see Adrian was moved by the message. He also appeared to be disturbed by something, my guess was what had happened to him earlier had stayed with him. I couldn't imagine what sort of thoughts he harbored toward that sergeant, or even the ire he felt in his heart having to suck up that verbal abuse.

I called to check on Chloe on my way home from work. Lately, she'd been acting distant, moping around the house and slacking on her chores. I'm sure a lot of it had to do with spending time worrying about the status of her relationship with Gabriel. His attitude toward her had changed; it was visible in the way she was acting. With teenagers, they wore their emotions on their sleeves so it wasn't too hard to see what had been affecting her.

Then again, it could be what was going on with Carl. To her, he could do no wrong, but his behavior lately had to be extremely upsetting to her. It was hard to watch your hero fall, and that was exactly what she had witnessed. Whatever the case, I hoped she was able to snap out of it before she went off to college. That had its own set of challenges and she didn't need any more distractions.

"Hey honey, how are things going?"

"Fine," she stated flatly.

"Anything new and exciting happen today at school?" I was trying to desperately break the icy tone in her voice.

"Look Mom, can you stop with all the Claire Huxtable talk?" I had to laugh, which caused her to chuckle.

"What you know about *The Cosby Show*? That was way before your time."

"As long as there is a channel that shows reruns, I catch up on everything you used to watch. Sometimes, I wish our family could've been like that." Her comment pierced my heart a bit.

"Me too, Chloe, but life isn't a television program where all the problems cease when the show goes off."

"With all the issues Bill Cosby has going on and the things Dad is going through, there are some similarities."

"Lighten up on your father, he's dealing with a lot."

"How can you defend him? And what about what I've been dealing with? We are the laughingstock of the school. My social life has gone straight to hell."

"Chloe!"

"I'm just saying. You asked what's going on, well I'm telling you how you and Dad's issues are affecting me."

I went ahead and let her vent; she had a right to express how she felt. The parents never intended for their situations to fall on their children; we sure didn't. Life had a way of splashing you with an ice cold glass of water. This was definitely a wakeup call to get our act together.

"Have you heard from Gabriel? How is he treating you?"

"I don't even want to talk about how he's been acting. All of a sudden, he has his head in the clouds. He doesn't talk about basketball or anything anymore. He says his mind is focused on getting his paper. What hurt me the most was him mentioning his newfound attraction for older women."

"Really?" I acted as if I was surprised, even though I remembered him flirting with me like he had no recollection for dating Chloe.

"Yeah, he says getting ready for college means preparing his mind for a new level with women. I felt so belittled, but he has his own life to live."

"Chloe, I'm sorry. I don't know why he did that to you," I tried to console her.

"It was like it happened overnight. One minute, he was all into his rehab, excited about his recovery, then it was a disappearing act, now this sudden urge to kick it with the Golden Girls." I had to hold back my laughter.

"Well, what about your college plans? You haven't mentioned much lately."

"I talked to Dad about it." I felt kind of excluded from her future.

"At first, we thought it would be good to stay close to home but as a result of all the negative publicity Dad is receiving, I may reconsider and get as far away from here as I can." That was disheartening to hear, but I could certainly understand her reasoning. Chloe was reaching adulthood, so it was important for her to make tough decisions. She just needed to know that her parents, no matter what they were going through, weren't too far away.

"Max, I'm worried that my family is falling apart."

When I got home and noticed Carl wasn't there, I took the time to relax and give my good friend a call. Normally, I'd head over to her office for a scheduled session, but this call was to my friend and not my therapist.

Maxine had been familiar with my story from the beginning. I remember when I was so nervous telling her about my sordid past and my unpleasant present. She always made me feel like I had a hopeful future. Those sessions became a platform that strengthened our bond. Max never judged me, nor did she give me advice that would be detrimental. Her observations were refreshing, which allowed me space to open up. Over time, we realized that talking was the best stress reliever and listening helped to heal.

When she went through her trials, I was honored to be the one she called on. It was evident that she didn't have too many people in her corner. Her family didn't even come to her aid. I often wondered why she seldom spoke about her family. Maybe it was because she had been let down one too many times. I definitely knew the feeling.

As we spoke, I peered out the blinds, surveying the neighborhood like I often did when I was on the phone. Usually, our neighbors were busying around in their little worlds, shuttling in and out of driveways, gardening, or washing cars. All activity seemed normal and I was about to close the blinds when I saw a suspicious, yet familiar vehicle driving slowly down our street.

At closer inspection, I noticed the driver and passenger got out after they parked across the street. One of the men, I recognized instantly from the caper Gabriel and I went on to acquire the money to help Max. The black SUV was the same one I'd been seeing around town, the same one I saw parked in front of that house. But why was it parked across the street from my house? Then I remembered that my car was sitting in our driveway. Could it be possible I was spotted leaving the scene? Had I brought these problems to my doorstep?"

"Cookie, are you still there? You got real quiet on me."

"Oh yeah...ah, I was looking out the window and something drew my attention."

"You okay? You sound a little rattled." I didn't know how to think at the moment. I watched them walking around different cars, looking at license plates then at house numbers. Nervousness filled the empty space in my stomach where my food used to be. In fact, vomiting was sounding pretty good at the moment.

"Max, did your lawyer tell you how to handle the situation with these guys?"

"What guys?"

"You know, the ones that gave you the money to change your story, the reason you went to jail?" I had to remind her with a harsh pill of the truth.

"Oh yeah, them," she replied as if they were the furthest thing from her mind. "He said that since I did the jail time, he didn't see them being a problem."

"How is that, Max? You took money from them. Did you think they wouldn't come looking for it?"

"I haven't seen or heard from them lately, I believe they have forgotten all about me."

"That may or may not be true but right now, they are in my neighborhood, across the street and I'm pretty sure they're looking for me."

"Looking for you? Why? You didn't do anything to them. In fact, I don't think they even know about you."

"Oh, I think they do. They're fishing around in my driveway now. Let me call you back, Max."

"Cookie, wait—" I ended the call and got away from the window.

Chloe was upstairs being antisocial, as usual. She didn't realize the impending danger we were in if those guys outside put two and two together, figuring out that it was my car that fled the scene after Gabriel shot up the place. I was sure he didn't leave anyone standing, but then again, how sure could I be when my adrenaline was on 1000?

Kind of like it was at the moment. I called up to Chloe three times, trying to alert her, but I got no response. More than likely, she was on one of her devices with the headphones on. This was precisely the reason our young generation was unaware of the world around them; technology had them in a fog.

The melody on my cell phone scared me to death, reminding me of how on edge I was. Looking down at the screen, I noticed it was Carl. His name itself brought a cadre of emotions; anger, comfort, uncertainty, security, bitterness, but in my present state, the Carl of old was who I hoped was on the call.

"Hello," I answered, praying he wouldn't detect anything in my voice.

"Sandra, I think we need to have a serious talk, just me and you. We should do it somewhere with no distractions. I just want an opportunity to get things back to where we used to be."

"Carl..."

"Please, hear me out, Sandra," he pleaded. His voice had a slight slur to it. I didn't want to suspect it, but I had to ask.

"Carl, have you been drinking?" I interrupted what seemed like his well-planned soliloquy.

"Why...ah, well a little bit. I've been sitting, thinking about everything going on and..."

"Where are you now, Carl?" I asked, still conscious of who was lurking outside.

"I'm on my way home so we can have a nice family dinner, I bought some things to cook." His sweet sentiment was overshadowed by my concern for our family's safety.

"Ah...you can't come home right now."

"What you mean? I live there, dammit! I pay the bills there, Sandra!" he shouted, taking things totally the wrong way.

"No, Carl you don't understand," I tried to reason with him.

"What you don't understand is that I'm on my way and that's final." He ended the call just as Adrian was calling in. His voice was so calm and comforting. I didn't know how to express how I was feeling. I missed talking to him and under normal circumstances, this time would be taken advantage of. These weren't normal circumstances.

"Hey, you!" he opened excitedly. "How's life treating you?"

"All bad, Adrian. I'm trying to manage a situation, doing the best I can."

"Anything I can do to help?"

"Wish you could. Being here could make it better." Just when I was ready to take my next breath, there was a knock on the door. Not a knock like the cops do when they're trying to show intimidation. No, this was more of a knock to inform whomever was inside that they knew someone was home. This knock was out of courtesy to those innocents, because the target of their attention was indeed home and knew exactly who was looking for them. I stood frozen in time, phone to my ear, just listening...

"Cookie, you still there?" There was nothing but silence on the other end of the call.

The end

Stay Tuned for part 3...

MALICE and MURDER

by

Sa'id Salaam

"And just what do we have here, Officer Malice?" Janine purred as she kissed her way down Detective Carl Malease's hairy chest.

He just shook his head at the nickname it looked like he was never going to shake. Especially not right now, with his coworker nearing his navel while gripping his thick erection. She knew he hated being called that and stifled a giggle before sticking her tongue in his belly button. He gave her head a nudge to move things along but it had the opposite effect.

"Don't be rushing me!" Janine fussed, and reminded him why their relationship never went any further than the sack.

She was a stallion, standing five feet, ten inches tall, with smooth yellow skin and long, curly hair. Classic urban fiction book looks on the arm of the kingpin. She did make a nice contrast to Malease's chestnut brown complexion. He had her by four inches when she was barefoot and naked, like now. The couple was never really a couple, even if they did have hot, steamy sex a couple times a month.

The detectives were both assigned to the Manhattan narcotics unit that battled the unending war on drugs. They weren't the only males or females in the unit checking for either of them but they ended up in each other's beds.Stakeouts can be boring and tedious so Janine broke the monotony one night by asking to see his dick. Carl Malease was very proud of what he had and promptly whipped it out. It was too pretty to just look at so she gave it a feel. A pat on the head like a puppy, then gripped it and watched it grow longer, thicker, and harder right there in her palm. She threw caution to the wind and pulled down her pants.

There wasn't much room in the car so she leaned over and let him slide in from behind. She didn't blame him for the quick nut since she knew she had some good pussy. Careful rationing of it kept it nice and right and tight. Plus, the excitement of fucking your partner in the front seat during a stakeout got the better of him.Later that morning, they'd traded places with the next shift and made a beeline to her Chelsey apartment. He wondered how she could afford to live there until he got her in bed. That squishy, hot box could pay rent, car notes and fund a 401k quite nicely.

The sex was mutually satisfying but they quickly realized it was all they had in common. Malease was a straight laced, by the book cop, looking to move up the ranks. Janine was as crooked as the other cops in the unit who were more concerned with how much they could skim.

Carl turned a blind eye to his comrades' skims and scams. This line of work could easily corrupt and he fought the daily battle of subtraction and percentages that filled his fellow detectives' pockets and offshore accounts. A three kilo bust always ended up one kilo after they got their share. A hundred grand seizure would be lucky to be thirty by the time they took their cuts. Unless Malease found it first. His comrades began to call him 'Malice' since that's what their crooked hearts harbored towards him. Most hoped he got killed in the line of duty so they could get rich. If he got the promotion he was bucking for they would go broke or to jail.

"Uh, you came over here," he reminded but left out the part about it being unannounced. She had popped up at his door knowing he intended to follow up on a lead. Some dummy was selling a variety of drugs via Instagram. He displayed pounds of this and ounces of that in his stories. When Malease saw the dangerous fentanyl, he decided to hit him up.

"Yeah, cuz you bugging. Leave that kid alone," she suggested and planted a loud kiss on the head of his dick.

It momentarily distracted him until he remembered what he was dealing with. "'That kid' is selling one of the most dangerous drugs on the planet. To other kids! 'That kid' just so happens to be the kid of Vincent Scalia. The drug kingpin Vincent Scalia. Same one we've been trying and failing to build a case on, for what? A decade!" he said and sat up as his dick went down.

"Malice, you can't really think this dumb kid actually works for his dad. He's a wannabe gangsta playing around," she said in his defense.

"He may not work for him but may want to help himself once I put cuffs on him," Malease said, revealing his plans.

"And what does Lieutenant have to say about this?

How come Velez hasn't briefed the rest of the team on this?" she demanded even though she knew the answer.

Carl Malease may have been straight laced and by the book but he didn't mind skipping a page or two when it suited him. He overlooked his own wrong in favor of the right that resulted. "I'm sure he'll see things my way," he shrugged. Carl now regretted even telling her about his plans. He should have waited until it was done and nothing could be done about it.

"Bruh, just chill with me. Get ya dick sucked. Get some of this," she said and pulled his hand between her legs, "good, hot pussy!"

"It is hot," he agreed and felt his dick jump as it began to come back alive.

She dipped her head and breathed her hot breath on it. It responded to its full glory in seconds. She took in the tip and eased him down her throat like an anaconda at dinner time.

Carl's dick had gotten him in trouble before but now it could keep him out of trouble. He fingered her bubbly box while she worked her lips and fingers like playing a flute. His mind was made up about blowing off the meet as he looked down and watched her blow his meat.

Then, the phone rang.

"Mm-mm," she hummed and shook her head from side to side.

Carl checked the caller ID and decided to take the

call. "Lil Vinny!" he greeted then grimaced when Janine deliberately scraped his dick with her teeth.

"Yeah, just checking to make sure youse guys are still coming? If not, I can sell this shit in school," the novice dope boy dared.

"Shit!" Carl said when he realized he wasn't going to enjoy her tonsils like planned. He pulled out of her mouth and rolled away. "I'm on my way. See you in a few. I want the whole brick!"

Janine's mouth was now empty, so she could only suck her teeth. She almost called out and called him 'Officer Malease' loud enough to be heard. That could get him killed though and that's not what she wanted. She would much rather he be safe and sound eight inches deep inside of her.

"I gotta bounce. Raincheck?" he asked as he dressed. He paused to hear her answer since he wanted to pick up where they left off after making this bust.

"I guess," she said ruefully and twisted her lips. Her mind raced on ways to stop him but came up with nothing. She could shoot him in his calf muscle but he would probably still go. One part of her admired his valor and honor but her other parts didn't.

"Good, cuz there's not a finer vagina north of South Carolina," he said, showing off his signature humor. It was part of why he was so well liked in the department. Even if his unit hated him.

"You so silly," Janine laughed and looked up like she was love struck. She could love him in another time and place. Maybe if they were doctors or philanthropists where they really could help and save people. But they were New York City narcotic detectives. Their job was to make as much money as possible without going to jail themselves.

"Yeah, ummm...." Malease suggested and raised an eyebrow since she was still stretched out on his bed.

"What? You don't want me to stay here and wait for you?" she purred and patted her kitty.

"Yeah right!" he laughed and she laughed with him. They may have screwed all over each other's apartments but no way would either leave the other alone in theirs.

"Oh alright," she sighed and rolled off the bed. She made sure to jiggle her lady parts as a last ditch effort to keep him home.

"I hear you," he said of the display and continued getting dressed for the deal. Being undercover meant he got to wear the clothes he would wear anyway. The city still sprang for a clothing allowance that allowed him to purchase high-priced sneakers and expensive jeans. Even the platinum chain, pendant and bracelet came courtesy of the tax payers.

"Malice saves the world," Janine quipped as they made their way through his apartment in a Bronx tenement building

"Detective Malease does his job," he corrected.

He would have kissed her had she leaned in for one.

She didn't, so they both went to their separate cars to go their separate ways. They both pulled out their phones and made calls.

"Yo, Little Vinny," Malease said when the nineteen-year-old answered his phone. "I'm on the way."

"Lieutenant, this is Polk," Janine said and paused. She didn't want to do what she was about to do but it had to be done.

"Yeah?" the unit lieutenant asked and began shaking his head already. If it was good news she wouldn't be calling. She would be giving some of that first class head that put those sergeant stripes on her arm. She was a good cop but not having gag reflexes paid huge dividends as well.

"He's on his way to meet him. I couldn't stop him," she reported.

"Shit! Follow him and keep me up to speed," he said and reached for his pants. He'd planned a nice quiet night with his mistress but tonight was going to be everything but quiet.

CHAPTER ONE

"You ready for the big leagues, Palo?" Little Vinny asked his sidekick in the passenger seat.

"Hells yeah!" the hype man hyped. He was to Little Vinny what Flavor Flav was to Chuck D since they wanted to be public enemies.

Little Vinny was the oldest son of the reputed mobster Vinny Scalia, the man who controlled a large portion of the dope, numbers, and pussy sold in the city. It was said if a crack addict gave a four dollar blow job up in the Bronx, two of those dollars came to him. In other words, he ran this city. Most kids would be content to just be related to boss of the city. He lived in a Westchester county mansion and fucked all the Spanish maids. He drove a souped up Mustang just like Tommy from *Power*, because he wanted to be Tommy from *Power*.

"A quick hun'ned grand," Vinny nodded as the car hugged the curves heading down to the city.

"Easy money!" the hype man hyped on cue. His small mind wondered what his cut might be, if he got a cut. Not that he minded either way since he benefited just by being the man next to the man.

If only Vinny could be so content.

He couldn't, though, and that's why he'd stolen a kilo of fentanyl from one of the stash spots. His dad turned a blind eye when he routinely swiped pounds of weed to sell to the rich kids. He knew the feeling that being the man brought and wanted his namesake to get a taste. Fentanyl was the big leagues now and he was in way over his head-.He'd advertised via IG and had several dealers to choose from. He chose the one who went by Malice BX because he liked the name. A hundred grand sale would have him flossing and fronting real good amongst his peers. Especially since no one really liked the obnoxious brat.

"Wish we had more! Like five. We could make a million!" Palo said, star struck by the idea.

"Ten times would be a million, you fucking moron!" Vinny laughed. He'd chosen him for his brawn not brains and did the thinking for the both of them.

"Oh yeah!" he laughed, even though he still didn't get it. A new thought quickly chased away the old one. "W-w-what if, if th-they try to r-r-rob us?"

"Who are you? P-p-p-porky fucking p-p-pig! You sound like a real bitch right now!" he said, sounding just like O-Dog from *Menace to Society*.That's because he wanted to be O-dog from *Menace to Society* as well. He watched all the gangsta movies and imitated all the main characters. That was fine in the mansion, but he was in the streets now.

He reached under the seat and pulled out a large fifty caliber weapon. "Try my gangsta and I got something for his ass!" Vinny proclaimed. The very feel of the gun threatened to make his dick hard. He had fired it plenty of times at the range but was itching to try it out in real life so he could make his bones by causing a real death. "As a matter of fact..."

"As a matter of fact, what?" Palo asked. The sinister look in his friend's eyes scared him to the core. He may have looked like he was built like that but that was from football and lacrosse. His muscular physique meant nothing in the streets. A scrawny twelve-year-old with a .25 caliber holds more weight than all the muscles in the world.

"Shoot, I could just rob his ass. Do that ten times, and that's my mil," Vinny plotted. He had heard rumors of how ruthless his father could be and wanted to be like him just as much as any of the other gangsters he looked up to.

"But, your dad has a ton of that stuff," Palo pleaded. He'd gone with him to the stash house and seen it for himself. Millions of dollars' worth of various types of drugs.

"Yeah but I'm my own man," Vinny said it like he

believed it. In truth, he was a jigsaw puzzle made up of characters from the movies. He was part Tommy, part O-Dog, and part Nino Brown. With a dash of Pesci, a sprinkle of De Niro and two tablespoons of Pacino. Plus, he was his parents' son and both Mr. and Mrs. Scalia were as gangsta as it gets.

"Hmm," Malease hummed as he scoped out the meeting place.

The abandoned dock was the perfect place to do anything and not be seen. A driver of a Benz was leaned back in his seat as a street worker worked her mouth below.Malease scanned the area for cameras and didn't see any. The seasoned vet actually preferred to do deals in public to prevent the fuck shit. It's hard to commit an armed robbery in the middle of Grand Central Station.

"This kid ain't 'bout dat life," he reminded himself as he got into character. Little Vinny was green enough to leave his account public even though he used it to traffic narcotics. Malease had perused Little Vinny's life and saw him with his famous father. He knew if he nailed the son, the father would fall.

Carl Malease was the product of a two-parent household where slang was never spoken. The family might converse in Spanish, Arabic or Bengali over dinner, but never slang. His mother was an educator until Allah took what belonged to him and called her home. The beautiful Bangladeshi woman added to his dark, exotic features.His dad was one of the most decorated narcotics cops in the history of the city. They called Carl Senior 'Malice' as well because of the way he hit the streets. He tore into the drug industry with pure malice and made a real impact. Carl was chasing his records despite the opposition of his team. He routinely lost a good percentage of his bust to their internal thievery. Once he made lieutenant, he would drain the swamp and start over.

"Showtime," Malease said when he heard the pipes of the Mustang before it rounded the corner.

"That's him?" Palo asked when he saw Malease posted up on the department Porsche.

"Gotta be," Vinny said and put the car in park.

He tucked the Desert Eagle into his back as he got out. Palo grabbed the bag containing enough fentanyl to kill a whole borough.

Hope you don't pull it, Malease thought when he saw him tuck the tool. He mentally touched the forty caliber on his hip for comfort. And nothing gives comfort in cold and uncertain times like the feel of cold steel.

The cop needed a clean arrest that would hold up to the meticulous lawyers the father would no doubt enlist. If it stood up, the father would be forced to deal. His love for his own family was legendary.

"Malice BX?" Vinny asked and spread a deceiving smile on his baby face.

"Word. You must be Vinny," he greeted back and checked them both out in an instant. The big guy was just big but fear seeped from his pores like sweat. He walked light like an unarmed person does and Malease quickly dismissed him as a threat.

"In the flesh. Now, let's see that bread!" he demanded.

"Sure, let's see the product," the undercover cop shot back.

Every fiber of his being tensed at the moment of truth. The hundred grand he'd brought for the deal was actually ten thousand of his own dollars since he couldn't secure buy money from the city. He made up the difference with prop money he'd purchased online. It worked fine for rappers to floss and toss in music videos but this was a drug deal. The department usually fronted some of the millions of confiscated dollars for undercover buys. This one wasn't sanctioned so he was on his own.

"Count that!" Vinny ordered when Malease passed the cash.

"Take a bump so I know that's the real deal," Malease dared.

The product was tripled wrapped and double sealed since it was so dangerous. "I wouldn't take a bump with his nose!" Vinny shot back and distracted his help.

Malease nodded at the right answer since no one in their right mind would take a hit of straight fentanyl.

"It's all here," Palo said, to Malease's surprise.

He'd planned to pounce the moment the fake money

was discovered. It would have been a done deal by then and he would have had them dead to rights.

There was a terse split second pause as both plotters plotted. Then, the guns came out.

"New York City Police! Show me your hands!" Malease screamed.

Things shifted to slow motion as Vinny came around his back with the huge gun. The cop didn't want to shoot but didn't want to get shot even more.

"Die, cop!" Vinny shouted as the gun came up.

Malease couldn't let him point the big barrel in his direction. He dipped into a shooter's stance and fired a round into the man's bicep. Palo had seen more than enough and took off running into the night.

"No, no, no!" Janine fussed as she watched the events unfold before her eyes. She got a good look at Palo as his run for his life took him right past where she was posted up.

"Drop it!" Malease shouted and kept his weapon trained at the critical center mass like they were trained to do in the academy. Time went back to normal speed and that's always a good sign that the danger has passed.

"Fuck you, cop!" the spoiled brat screamed. "Do you know who I am? Who my father is?"

"Drop the weapon, kid. I'm not going to tell you again!" the cop shouted. It wasn't true though because he would have told him a thousand times rather than shoot him again. He needed the son alive to make a case against the father

Vinny huffed and puffed with the heavy gun still in his badly damaged arm. Malease knew if he continued to bleed at that rate, he would be an empty shell in a minute. The kid couldn't raise his arm to point the gun if he wanted to. He wanted to, though, and reached for it with his other hand.

"Noooo!" Malease shouted as time slowed once again.

He waited for the last possible second before popping off two rounds that knocked the kid's life right out the big holes in his back.

"Officer needs assistance! Send a bus, I got one perp down!" he screamed into his radio even though Little Vinny was beyond anything an ambulance could do. A quick check of his pulse confirmed what he already knew. His open eyes stared off at whatever it is that dead people look at. Perhaps their spot in heaven or hell.

Malease stood up from the dead and looked around for the living. He scanned the area looking for Palo but he was halfway to Harlem by then. He would have run all the way back to Westchester if he had to. He would have had to if he hadn't come across the Metro North train when he finally reached 125th Street.

"What the fuck, Malease!" Janine groaned when she arrived with her gun drawn. Malease's eyes went wide as if he saw a ghost when he saw her. She had a million questions, but he only had one.

"What are you doing here?" he asked painfully.

"I followed you, duh!" she shot back. She leaned down to check Vinny's wrist and got the same results he got. "He's gone."

"He drew down on me. I tried not to shoot but he wouldn't put it down," he said and sighed.

She knew that already since she saw it unfold. "Yeah, but you weren't even supposed to be here! Lieutenant told you to leave it alone!" she reminded. She even offered her entire body to dissuade him away from this bust.

"This kid had a kilo of fentanyl! I wasn't letting it go! You can tell Lieutenant to kiss my ass!" he said in his own defense.

"Looks like you can tell him yourself," she said when their boss pulled up.